ABBOT DAGGER'S ACADEMY
AND THE QUEST FOR THE HOLY GRAIL

Sam Llewellyn is the author of many quite brilliant books for adults and children, including three about the delightful Darling children and two about Death Eric, the world's favourite rock genius.

D0928958

ABBOT DAGGER'S ACADEMY

AND THE QUEST FOR THE
HOLY GRAIL

SAM LLEWELLYN

PUFFIN

PUFFIN BOOKS

Published by the Penguin Group
Penguin Books Ltd, 80 Strand, London WC2R ORL, England
Penguin Group (USA) Inc., 375 Hudson Street, New York, New York 10014, USA
Penguin Group (Canada), 90 Eglinton Avenue East, Suite 700, Toronto, Ontario, Canada M4P 2Y3
(a division of Pearson Penguin Canada Inc.)
Penguin Ireland, 25 St Stephen's Green, Dublin 2, Ireland (a division of Penguin Books Ltd)
Penguin Group (Australia), 250 Camberwell Road, Camberwell, Victoria 3124, Australia
(a division of Pearson Australia Group Pty Ltd)
Penguin Books India Pvt Ltd, 11 Community Centre, Panchsheel Park, New Delhi – 110 017, India
Penguin Group (NZ), 67 Apollo Drive, Rosedale, North Shore 0632, New Zealand
(a division of Pearson New Zealand Ltd)
Penguin Books (South Africa) (Pty) Ltd, 24 Sturdee Avenue, Rosebank,
Johannesburg 2196, South Africa

Penguin Books Ltd, Registered Offices: 80 Strand, London WC2R ORL, England

puffinbooks.com

First published 2008
1

Text copyright © Sam Llewellyn, 2008
All rights reserved

The moral right of the author has been asserted

Set in Baskerville MT
Typeset by Palimpsest Book Production Limited, Grangemouth, Stirlingshire
Made and printed in England by Clays Ltd, St Ives plc

British Library Cataloguing in Publication Data
A CIP catalogue record for this book is available from the British Library

ISBN: 978-0-141-32172-1

For the great John Wells,
who taught me French

Welcome to the Badlands.

The Badlands is a nasty place, full of nasty animals. There are woewolves, whose bite is certain blood poisoning. There are blunderbuffaloes, tenton carnivorous giants that will sit on you as soon as look at you and eat you when they get up. There is all kinds of bad stuff.

Across the Badlands there slants a valley: a deep. wild valley with a black river writhing along its green bottom, reflecting just at the moment bloody lights from a storm-wrecked sunset.

In a loop of the river stand buildings: a tower, a cloister and a sprawl of others, set among muddy fields spiked with goalposts. Lights burn in pointed windows, and a cold wind wails in the gargoyles on the tower. It looks like a school. A school is what it is: a boarding school, in fact.

Its ancient buildings are rambling and crumbling. Its modern buildings are stark and vile. For hundreds of years, they have been crammed with children who did not fit in anywhere else. There were ordinary non-fitter-ins, called Skoolies. And there were rather more brilliant ones, called Skolars. They were all somewhat special, in their ways.

For example:

Swami Barmi was a Skoolie, and nobody made any remarks about him floating around in mid-air during lessons. El Vulpo, later the terrible Dictator of Nananagua, was a Skoolie too, Captain of Footbrawl, and nobody found him all that tough. And Professor Igor Startoff, when he was a Skolar, converted the Skool central heating to atomic power without anyone thinking he was anything special.

Basically, Abbot Dagger's is a Skool for children so weird or so bad or so just plain brilliant that they need to be taken far from civilization and fenced in by a river in front (there is one of them) and a cliff behind (there is one of them too). Abbot Dagger's Academy for the Errant Children of the Absent, its staff call it. Its pupils call it Bad Skool, or just Skool.

So here we are. At the beginning of a story, at the beginning of the autumn term . . .

Hang on.

Up in the Badlands the animals suddenly stop eating each other and cock their loathsome heads as if listening. They are indeed listening, but to thoughts, not words. Woewolves howl and clash their greenish fangs. Blunderbuffaloes twitch their bucket-sized nostrils as if scenting blood. They listen closely to what seems to be . . . a summons. Then they lick their awful teeth and lope towards the Edge, where the road leaves the Badlands and plunges into the valley, heading straight as an arrow for the drawbridge that is the only access to the Skool.

Interesting, the animals seem to be thinking.

Trouble. Lots of it.

Yum yum.

1

'What very interesting children these do sound!' said Solomon Temple, vague, lovable Headmaster of Abbot Dagger's Academy.

'I hate interesting children, sss,' said Dr Cosm, severe, grim Head of Behaviour and Physics. 'Give me the report cards. Let us see them in cold print.'

'Say please,' said the Headmaster, shocked.

Cosm fixed him with a cold and jellied eye. 'No,' he said, and reached out a wet white hand, and pulled the cards towards him.

ROSETTI SVENSON

Age: 12

IQ: 170

Star sign: Pisces

Background: Parents international art thieves. Father has worked as a painter and lion tamer. Mother was principal dancer with the

4

Mariinsky Ballet, then proprietor, Mrs Svenson's Performing Hyenas, and the Svenson Gallery, Swish Street, Mayfair. Present whereabouts of parents unknown. No brothers or sisters. Educated in the capitals of Europe and at nineteen schools.

Talents: Drawing, English, running, Communication with People and Animals.

Crimes: Lack of respect for Authority. Use of animal languages to overthrow order and discipline. An enthusiastic prankster, inventor of the Electric Apple-Pie Bed and the Whitewash Milkshake.

Regime: Award Skolarship. Watch closely.

OWEN FRENCH

Age: 12

IQ: 230 (machine broke)

Star sign: Virgo

Background: Parents run the Post Office, Lesser Twittering, Hampshire. Seeking the best for their child they handed him over to the police on his eighth birthday.

The police handed him back two days later, claiming that he had beaten them all at chess and poker and they could not stand him one minute longer. No known emotions. Twenty-three schools.

Talents: Mathematics, card games, Chess Grand Master, mechanical genius.

Crimes: Lack of respect for Authority in cases where he thinks Authority is not being logical. Blind obedience to Authority (the command 'Blow up some balloons' resulted in an explosion that totally wrecked St Wid's Primary, Stromforth).

Regime: Award Skolarship. Watch closely.

ONYX KEENE

Age: 11 $^{15}/_{16}$ ths

IQ: Machine was mended but broke again

Star sign: Twinkly

Background: Parents university lecturers engaged in research into Ancient Pomeranian civilizations, early languages and the Theory

of Everything. They are wrapped up
in their work. This caused Onyx
to learn twenty-eight extra
languages in the hope that her
parents would agree to talk to her
in one of them.
Talents: Languages, research,
history.
Crimes: Excessive keenness. Awful,
dreadful, maddening keenness.
Regime: Award Skolarship. Watch
closely.

'See, Cosm?' said the Head, rubbing his hands. 'So
mysterious! So logical! Such keenness! What could
be better in a set of Skolars?'

Cosm sniffed. 'Good behaviour,' he said. 'Total
obedience. A humble outlook. Full marks in all
Tests.'

'You and your Tests!' cried the Head, ignoring
the look of hatred Cosm flung at him. 'All that
matters is that everyone be happy and learn lots!'

'Hopelessly unscientific,' said Cosm, and sniffed
again.

The Head smiled encouragingly, for he was a
kind and cheerful man. But he did hate Cosm's
sniffing. And his Tests.

And actually most of the rest of him too.

*

Onyx Keene had said goodbye to her mummy and daddy as fast as possible. Now she was sitting on the edge of her chair in the Hall of Session. She was very, very excited. She had been awarded a Skolarship to Abbot Dagger's! And today she had met the Headmaster! Well his knees anyway, because she was not tall and the Headmaster was, very! The knees had been baggy and dusty as if he had been looking for something under a sofa! And here she was at Skool which was what you had to call it! And there were twelve Skolars in her year but only three Polymathic ones which were the best kind because Onyx was one, and all Skolars had to live in a part of the Skool called the Skolary which was incredibly ancient, and Polymathic meant that you were good at a lot of things not just one or two things, and Onyx wondered whether they had blankets or duvets in the dorms and what was for supper and where the Library was and she could hardly *wait*!

The Hall of Session at Abbot Dagger's Academy was an enormous room with a stage at one end. Facing the stage were 201 children wearing the Skool uniform of tailcoats and striped trousers for boys, tailcoats and long striped skirts for girls. In the middle of the stage stood the Head with his long white hair and his long black gown and his dirty knees. Behind him was a semicircle of chairs occupied by more teachers. On either side of the stage, hands clasped behind their backs, stood two stocky men in the black uniform of Security, their hard eyes scanning the crowd for trouble.

'Ahem,' said the Head. 'We will sing the Skool Song. Pupils be upstanding!'

A huge chord rolled into the hall. Onyx started bouncing in her seat. She *loved* singing! *Particularly* Skool Songs! Up she stood. Up everyone stood.

> 'WE HAVE NOT BEEN VERY GOOD,' sang the
>   Skool.
> 'WE HAVE NOT DONE RIGHT.
> WE HAVE BEEN MISUNDERSTOOD
> AND SET OUR SCHOOLS ALIGHT,
> BUT OUR HEARTS ARE VERY HIGH,
> PROUD AND CLEAN ARE WE.
> O YES WE ARE HAPPY NOW
> AT OUR AKADEMEE.
> DAGGA DAGGA DAGGA DAGGA
> SKOOL-A-SKOOL-A-SKOOL-A-SKOOL!'

Dead insects fell out of the rafters. The children sat down.

'Welcome to the summer term at Abbot Dagger's Academy!' cried the Head.

Kind eyes! thought Onyx.

'And welcome to our New People.'

That's nice! thought Onyx.

'Now, then. I know you are all here because no

other school in the kingdom will have you.' He smiled a kindly smile. 'But here we are and we must make the best of it. Now I must introduce the staff. I am the Headmaster, natch.'

Clapclapclap*clap*, went Onyx.

'Suck,' hissed the barrel-shaped girl in front of her, flicking a lit match in her general direction.

'Hangyou, too kind, simmer down,' said the Head, kind eyes twinkling. 'Now, a trip to the Dark Side. Take a bow, Dr Cosm (Behaviour and Physics)!'

Dr Cosm stood up, and trained upon the pupils eyes like holes burned in a large white pudding. A ripple of fear ran through the ranks.

Oo, nasty! thought Onyx.

'Hangyou hangyou,' said the Head. 'Siddown, Cosm.' He introduced a mob of geography teachers, maths teachers, civics teachers and French teachers, speaking in a gabble as if anxious to get it over with. 'Next, Matron, otherwise known as Nurse Drax, dangerous woman, don't mess.' Nurse Drax had red lips and redder eyes. She stood up, then sat down. A happier expression spread over the Head's face. 'Wrekin Sartorius, art,' he said. 'Talented man, needs a haircut. And last but not least a new addition. Boys and girls, I am proud to present to you Miss Artemisia Davies, who has joined us after a period with the Consorority of Ipsissimi. Miss Davies is an Old Dagger, which means she used to be a pupil here, so there are no flies on her, except when she is wearing trousers, haha.'

'Oo, *funny*!' squealed Onyx.

'Haha,' roared all the other children.

Miss Davies was quite young and very pretty, with curly blonde hair, tawny skin and eyes that reminded Onyx (who knew just about everything) of topazes. She smiled at Onyx kindly. Singling her *out*! 'Miss Davies is the new Polymathic Skolars Tutor,' said the Head. 'Or perhaps I should say Skolar, because the other two Skolars are late, which means sadly that they have probably been eaten by wild animals.'

It is my first day and I have already been *mentioned*! thought Onyx, noticing for the first time that there was an empty chair on either side of her.

The Head beamed again. 'Well, children, I am sure that like me you are getting very, very bored with all this. You will find all the usual guff on the Skool noticeboard. All that remains is for me to say that Founder's Day will be the first Saturday after the full moon in October, i.e. in five weeks' time. Assembly, dis–'

But before he could finish, an enormous bell began to ring from the lofty building known as the Tower of Flight. 'Wha?' said Onyx to the barrel-shaped match girl, who seemed to be called Elphine.

'It's the intruder bell,' said the stout girl. 'Signal

of danger. This way!' The hall rang with mighty cheers and the thunder of boots on ancient flagstones. Onyx ran after the crowd at top speed. It stopped on a small hill overlooking the gate of the Academy. Being small for her age, she was able to creep to the front without being much harmed. 'Lower the drawbridge!' cried the Head. 'The station bus has arrived!'

Down came the bridge over the swift-flowing Water of Darkness. Across it there trundled an armoured steam bus of the kind used to collect pupils from the station. Or rather the wreckage of an armoured steam bus. The driver's cab was empty, the engine silent. The reason the bus was moving was that it was being pulled by a team of sixteen vast horned animals that Onyx instantly recognized as blunderbuffaloes. The beasts were being driven by a lanky boy with floppy brown hair and a faraway expression, sitting on the cab roof. He had no whip and no reins. But Onyx got the idea that he was . . . *making suggestions* . . . to the enormous animals. And beside him sat a huge grey doglike animal with its tongue hanging out. 'Goodness me,' said someone, taking a couple of steps backwards. 'It's a woewolf.'

Beside the woewolf sat another boy, this one with spiky blond hair. The spiky boy was looking at the Skool buildings in much the same way that a digital camera looks at a football team.

'Hooray!' cried the Head, beaming. 'Our missing Polymathic Skolars have arrived.'

My fellow Skolars! thought Onyx, lasering them with her eyes. How *thrilling*!

But Dr Cosm broke in, in a voice like a jet of lemon juice. 'Clearly these wicked pupils have attacked the driver and locked him in the bus, whose engine they have destroyed! Security, prepare the Punishment Cells!'

'Um,' said the Head.

There was a rather embarrassing silence. It was broken by the voice of Miss Artemisia Davies, Tutor to the Polymathic Skolars. 'Perhaps that's not what happened,' said Miss Davies. 'Why don't we ask them?'

'Good idea,' said the Head. Then, raising his voice, 'I say! Boys! What happened? Where's the driver?'

'The bus went off the road,' said the spiky-haired boy. 'The driver hid in the Pupil Compartment.'

'Impossible!' cried Dr Cosm.

A mournful face appeared behind the bars of the Pupil Compartment. Above it was a peaked cap bearing a badge that said DRIVER. 'It is all true,' said the face in a low, humble voice. 'We crashed. In the Badlands. Wild wild animals everywhere. The main cylinder blew. Naturally the animals turned up hopin' to eat us like. But this here Rosetti Svenson tamed 'em, using the mind. Let me out now, there's good lads.' The spiky boy pressed buttons and the pupil cage snapped open. 'Thankee, young sir,' said the driver. 'They're good boys, Head and Dr Cosm. Well, tough, anyway.'

The two boys slid from the bus's roof on to its bonnet, and from the bonnet on to the ground. 'Morning,' said the spiky-haired one to the Headmaster. 'I'm Owen. You must be the Head.'

'True,' said the Head, beaming. 'And this is Rosetti?'

'I wouldn't talk to him if I were you, not while he's talking to the animals,' said Owen.

Rosetti was standing by the foremost blunderbuffalo. There was a faraway look in his eyes. 'Off you go, and thanks a lot,' he murmured.

The blunderbuffaloes mooed. They turned towards the gate, lowered their heads and charged. There was a crash and a cloud of splinters. 'An exciting new project for Carpentry II,' said the Head musingly.

The woewolf grinned, showing jagged greenish teeth, and vanished – something woewolves tend to do.

'It looks to me as if the Skolars are complete,' said the Head. 'Miss Davies?'

'Of *course*!' said Miss Davies, who (Onyx now noted) had really beautiful bronze-coloured fingernails and perfect make-up. 'Come to the Skolary and I'll show you round.'

As they left the courtyard, they were followed by the amazed stares of the whole Skool, and the scowls of two large boys with shaved heads, battered noses and sweatshirts that said Skool Footer – Top Pair. Rosetti could feel their hot little eyes on his neck. 'Who are they?' he said to Miss Davies.

SLEE AND DAMAGE DUGGAN
Age: 12
IQ: 80 (combined)
Star sign: The Rhinoceros
Background: Parents, father Barry Duggan, bulldozer manufacturer and Parent Governor. Mother Iris Duggan, Northern Lard Queen 1998. These identical twins are at the Academy because their parents want them to be here – a very rare thing.
[NOTE ON FILE FROM DR COSM: Excellent. Fine, fine people.]
[NOTE ON FILE FROM HEADMASTER: It is a mystery how people this stupid can feed themselves without help.]
Crimes: ~~Incredible stupidity~~ Perfect obedience. Splendid pupils unsurpassed in any way by anyone. Great things are expected of them!

Also Barry Duggan, a very rich
man, gives the Academy enormous
amounts of money.
Regime: Pamper and cherish. Give
benefit of doubt at all times.

'The Duggan twins. Slee and Damage. Pure meat
from the shoes up. The opposite of Polymathic
Skolars, really. Now come along.' She led them
through a gate. 'OK,' she said, 'We are in the Main
Quadrangle. Explain what you see. Eyes shut, of
course.'

'Of course,' said Owen, lowering his lids. 'On
the right, a white wall with no windows. Ahead, a
tower with four hundred and eleven windows,
seventy-three of them quite small. On the left, a
line of eighty-one pillars with a covered walkway
with doors leading off it, another floor on top,
twenty-seven windows neatly arranged.'

'Are you by any chance a little autistic?' said Miss
Davies.

'No,' said Owen. '*Very* autistic.'

'Cool,' said Miss Davies. 'Now. Somebody else.
Onyx?'

Onyx had been bouncing up and down for some
time, eyes *shut tight*. She knew! She *knew*! 'On the
right, that white wall, is a modern building that I
have heard about designed by an architect called
Walter Strunk who went mad and did not believe

16

in windows. The thing up ahead is the Great Orrery with a working model of the planets powered by clockwork wound by water. And that high thing behind it is the Tower of Flight which is part of the original buildings erected by the first Abbot Marchmont Dagger in 1568 no 1569 I would have to check that in the library which is up there too I am very very keen on libraries. And to the left is the Cloister, built for contemplative walking, with doors leading to classrooms dormitories observatories and the Skool grounds. Behind us, of course, is the Hall of Session, where assemblies are held. Did I miss anything out?'

Miss Davies's mind appeared to have wandered. She came back to herself with a slight start. 'Probably not,' she said. 'Are you autistic too?'

'No,' said Onyx. 'Just *keen!*'

Miss Davies gave her a strained smile. 'Rosetti?' she said.

Rosetti shrugged. 'It's a school,' he said.

'Quite right!' said Miss Davies. 'Now, time for cocoa and buns!'

She led the way at a brisk trot into the building at the end of the quad. There was a great arched doorway. At the top of the arch was a carving of a monk's head with a dagger between its teeth. 'Abbot Dagger,' said Miss Davies. 'The founder.'

Inside the door was a warren of ancient rooms. There was a common room, with a huge coal fire and a seething mob of Skoolies who paid the new Skolars absolutely no attention. There were little bedrooms called dorms, each with two cots, a desk and a bookshelf. And there was a Study, containing three desks, panelled in blackest oak heavily carved. There was a blackboard. Over the blackboard hung scale models of mythical beasts. 'Your names have been painted on your lockers in gold paint because the Head is very keen on you,' said Miss Davies. 'And your dorms. Owen and Rosetti, you're in together. Onyx, you've got a dorm to yourself.'

'Oo!' said Onyx, absent-mindedly, for she was already reading a book. 'How *thrilling*!'

At lunch, Onyx sat next to barrel-shaped Elphine. 'Hello,' said Onyx.

'Shutcher face,' said Elphine.

'Why so nasty?' said Onyx, more puzzled than hurt.

'Because I'm a Skoolie and you're a Skolar and Skoolies hate Skolars because they're feeble,' said Elphine, nicking a handful of Onyx's chips. 'You got here because you are half crazy with extra brains. I got here the ordinary way.'

'What's that?'

'I went to an ordinary school but it was boring and it caught fire. Then I went to another ordinary school but the food was bad and it caught fire.

Then I went to another school but I didn't like it and it caught fire. Then they sent me here and people I hate catch fire.'

'What a terrible lot of *acc*idents!' said Onyx, filled with sympathy.

'Who said anything about accidents?' said Elphine, rattling a box of matches dreamily by her ear. 'I think I might be beginning to hate you a bit.'

In a desperate attempt to change the subject, Onyx said, 'So what's it like here?'

'It's cool,' said Elphine. 'They let me run the fire brigade.'

After lunch, everyone seemed to have places to go, and went. The Skolars didn't. Rosetti said, 'Let's explore.'

First they went down to the Water of Darkness, which was fast, deep and unswimmable. Away from the river, a cliff of black rock rose vertically from a playing field on which two mud-caked teams were struggling in a heap.

'The cliff is called the New Boy's Leap,' said one of the players, who had small eyes, a tattooed head and very few teeth. 'Because New Boys usually climb up it hoping to escape, find they can't go no further and jump off. Try it, Skolar.'

'You are trying to make us frightened,' said Owen.

'Yerse. Hur, hur.' A ball bounced across the field.

The boy lumbered after it. A thin cold rain began to fall.

This is a really terrible place, thought Rosetti, peering through the drizzle at the looming buildings.

'Perhaps there'll be a really fabulous library,' said Onyx, but even she did not feel much like bouncing when she said it. Owen said nothing, being busy watching an ant.

Back in the Study, Owen pulled out two chess sets and played Onyx and Rosetti at the same time. He checkmated Rosetti in three moves. He was on the point of finishing Onyx in five when the clock struck two, the door opened and Miss Davies came in.

'Greetings, Skolars!' she cried. 'Now tell me what is a Polymath? Yes, Onyx?'

'Someone who knows a lot about a lot of different things,' said Onyx.

'True, in a way,' said Miss Davies. 'And the motto of a Polymath?'

'Dunno,' said Owen.

'Rosetti?'

'Sorry?' said Rosetti, miles away.

'Onyx? Stop *bouncing*.'

'Sorry,' said Onyx. 'Ummmmmmm –'

'*There is more than one explanation for everything*,' said Miss Davies. 'Everything interesting, that is. The whole of Polymathic Studies is based on this idea.

Now. We have an appointment with the Head after his Governors' Meeting.'

This Governors' Meeting was being a difficult one. They all were. For the Governors really admired Dr Cosm, except for Inkon Stimp R.A., and nobody paid any attention to *him*. Part of the reason was that most of the Governors had once had children at the Skool, and none of them had been Skolars, so they were very jealous of the Polymathics, and hated the Head because the Polymathics were his favourite pupils. The other reason was that the Governors believed in Tests, and so did Cosm, but the Head thought Tests were stupid and childish.

'Founder's Day, plans for,' said Colonel De'ath, Chairman. 'Bit of marchin', what?'

'Discipline,' said Police Commissioner Bruce Manacle.

'And sports,' said Barry Duggan, Parent Governor. 'Lashin's of sports.'

'Plus Tests, of course,' said Professor Tube. 'Dr Cosm will take care of that. Good man, Cosm.'

'Wonderful man,' said Lady Squee.

'Sound fellow,' said Colonel De'ath.

'Solid citizen,' said Commissioner Manacle.

'Ahem,' said the Headmaster. 'We will of course be awarding the Greyte Cup for Running, Hard Sums and Lovely Writing.'

'Unless you've sold it,' said Colonel De'ath, who had no faith in the Head.

'Which would be a criminal offence,' said Commissioner Manacle, who had less.

'Shocking!' said Lady Squee, who despised everyone.

'But not unlikely,' said Professor Tube, sniffing. Since Cosm had arrived the year before, the Professor had become his biggest fan and longed to see him as Head.

'Writin'? Pafetic,' said Barry Duggan, slow on the uptake as always.

'Er . . .' said Inkon Stimp nervously.

'Gosh is that the time already?' said the Headmaster, looking at the wrong wrist. 'Now. Meeting closed. Busy schedule.'

'Look here, Headmaster,' said the Colonel. 'It's time your Polymathic whatsits proved themselves. If they don't win the Cup, you'll be looking for a new job. All Governors agree that Dr Cosm is right when he says the only way to deal with pupils like yours is Tests, Tests and more Tests. These Polymathic people may be very clever and all that but what good is cleverness if you don't test it? Eh? What? So if they don't win the Cup, you're sacked. Assuming the Cup is there to win and you haven't pawned it to get some money to bet on a horse. If the Cup's not there, obviously you're sacked anyway.'

'Hear, hear,' said all the other Governors, except

Inkon Stimp, who had lost interest some time ago and was drawing a rude picture of Dr Cosm's nose.

Casting looks of suspicion and dislike at the Head, the Governors stumped out of the room.

'Dear me,' said the Head as the door closed. 'That didn't go very well.' He rummaged in his desk and brought out a tin of delicious biscuits. 'Not very well at all. Ah, well.' He cleared his throat. 'Polymathic Skolars, enter!'

Rosetti's last headmaster had been a bit like a thundercloud full of sarcasm instead of rain. Once inside the massive oak door of the Study he looked around the room for a tall, scowling person with narrow eyes and a thin mouth. All he saw was the kindly white-haired man who had met them at the Skool gate.

'How I hate Governors,' said the white-haired man. 'Oh. Hello. Sit down, do. Biscuit?'

'Don't mind if I do,' said Rosetti.

'Take two,' said the Headmaster. 'Three. Stuff yourselves. Good biscuits. Otherwise the food's ghastly: nothing I can do – it's that Matron – pass them round.'

Rosetti passed them round. This was a kind of headmaster much, much nicer than the kind of headmaster he was used to. Miss Davies introduced everyone.

'Well, well, well, *strabonipticon hamash zingari*,' said the Headmaster.

'Wrong language,' said Miss Davies. 'Ancient Chaldean.'

'He says congratulations!' said Onyx. 'I *understood*!'

'Ah,' said the Head, resisting the urge to bean her with a cushion. 'Yes, welcome. Polymathic Skolars are my favourite people. I long for you to make a good impression. I should be so grateful if you could try to make, ah, one.'

'We will!' cried Onyx, bouncing again. 'We'll try soooo hard –'

'But actually it probably won't work,' said Owen.

Rosetti looked at keen Onyx and honest Owen and the slightly frantic Headmaster and felt a new emotion. He felt . . . *sorry* for the Head. 'It'll be fine,' he said.

'What a relief,' said the Head. 'We're all going to have a simply lovely time. And I know you will be a credit to me and to Polymathy.'

'Yes!' cried Onyx. 'We will, we will, won't we?!'

'S'pose,' said Owen and Rosetti. But as they filed out of the Headmaster's study, they were pondering deeply.

They had never met a Head like this. A really nice one, who gave you delicious biscuits. To their astonishment, they found they *really wanted* to be a credit to him.

They were just not quite sure how it was done.

Up near the ceiling, the little eye of a CCTV camera wheezed as the lens changed focus.

Far away in a white room filled with screens, a voice said, 'Pah! Insects! Those who frustrate me must prepare to be crushed!'

But of course they did not hear any of that.

2

Tea was in the Hall of Session. There were large buns with currants in, and milk that tasted like glue. Onyx tucked in eagerly. Owen munched steadily. Rosetti was reading a book. He took a small bite, looked up from his book, leaned back in his chair and snapped his fingers at Matron, who was prowling between the long tables. Matron stopped, her black eyebrows drawing together over her great hook nose. 'Wha,' she said, emitting fumes of gin.

'These are revolting,' said Rosetti, making a gesture at the milk-bun combo on his tray. 'Take them away and bring something better.' He went back to his book.

Matron smiled, revealing teeth like lipsticky piano keys. 'And what would you like, your lordship?' she cooed. 'Tart de apples in the French manner?'

'That would be fine,' said Rosetti, without looking up. 'By the way, I feel it is only a kindness to tell you that you smell.'

Matron's mouth fell open with a click.

'Of gin and cigarettes. Which are bad for you, so I'd give up if I were you. Now run along, chop chop.'

'Oo,' said Nurse Drax, by which she meant tick, tock, as in time bomb.

'Faster the better,' said Rosetti.

BOOM, went Matron. 'WHO DO YOU THINK YOU ARE TALKING TO YOU 'ORRIBLE SMELLY UNWASHED GOUR-MET SIR OR SHOULD I SAY YOUR LORDSHIP? YOUR LADIDA FRIEND THE HEADMASTER MAYBE. SO I SMELL IS IT WELL LET ME TELL YOU YOU ARE NO BED OF ROSES YOURSELF IN THE NIFF DEPARTMENT AND IF YOU DO NOT LIKE YOUR LOVELY BUNS AND NOURISHING MILK THERE IS BREAD AND WATER AND IT IS OVER HERE PREFECTS PREFECTS TAKE HIM TO THE CELLS!'

And before Rosetti knew where he was, he was in a small stone room without windows, gazing at a pottery jug of water and a round loaf with flecks of mould on it.

Hmm, thought Rosetti. Have I been a credit to the Headmaster?

Probably not.

*

Owen and Onyx watched their fellow Skolar carted away by beefy Prefects.

'What happens now?' said Onyx.

'Whole Skool New Term Quiz Test,' said Elphine the Match Girl.

A girl came round handing out paper. Everyone groaned.

'Quiz? Goodee,' said Onyx, beginning to bounce.

'Ik, swot,' said Elphine.

The questions flopped in front of the pupils. Owen started writing so fast that smoke rose from his pen.

To his left, a huge bulk shut out the light. ''Ello,' said the huge bulk. 'I Slee Duggan. I come sit with you.' To his right, another huge bulk shut out some more of the light.

''Ello,' said the other huge bulk. 'I Damage Duggan. I come to sit with you too. On other side like.'

'Cos we no can do them Test questions,' said Slee.

'An' we seen you done yours,' said Damage.

'So we've come to copy,' they said together.

Owen looked left. He looked right. Both Duggans had dirty ears and peg-toothed grins. He said, 'No.'

The grins vanished. 'Wot?' said the Duggans.

'You must obviously do the Test yourselves,' said

Owen. 'Or there is no point anyone setting them. Ow!' For the Duggans had lifted up his feet, and the floor had shot up to smack him on the back of the head.

On the dais, the Security Master stopped pacing. His eyes lasered across the room. 'Who's that?' he barked.

'He means you,' hissed the Duggans.

Owen stood up. He was too brilliant to be frightened, and much too autistic. 'It was me,' he said to the master. 'Owen French. Polymathic Skolar. I have finished the questions and got them all right. Now I want to go.'

'Go?' barked Security. 'I think that could be arranged, hur hur. PREFECTS PREFECTS!'

''Ere,' said Elphine the Match Girl, batting her eyelashes at Slee Duggan. 'I fancy you.'

Before Owen knew where he was, he was in a small stone room with no windows, gazing at a pottery jug of water and a round loaf of bread with green bits on it, and Rosetti, relaxing on a plank bed.

'How kind of you to join me!' said Rosetti.

'These people are bad,' said Owen.

'And obviously they will suffer,' said Rosetti, charming as ever. 'Now, then. Some bread? A little water?'

'Hmm,' said Owen, dragging the bread towards him and pulling out his Swiss Army knife.

Had he been a credit to the Headmaster?

The idea did not even cross his mind.

Onyx had seen Owen go, and she was actually a bit worried, and a bit lonely, because Elphine was now sitting with Slee Duggan and feeling his arm muscles admiringly. So she did the quiz, then waited until everyone had finished, passing the time by setting a few extra questions and answering them herself and then colouring in the loops of the letters. The Security Master had left the stage, to be replaced by the suet-faced Dr Cosm. 'Right,' said Cosm. 'Collect up papers. Whose turn?'

This was not the sort of question Onyx could leave unanswered. She felt herself swamped by waves of keenness. 'Me!' she cried, shooting her hand so high in the air that all her bones cracked. 'Me me me me meeeeee!' Then she realized all eyes were upon her, and turned bright red.

Among the eyes that landed on her were Dr Cosm's, small and black as frozen currants. He said, 'And who might you be, sss?'

'Onyx Keene sir sir please sir. A Skolar sir sir.'

Everyone was staring now. Onyx felt a sort of hollow feeling that she did not recognize. It seemed to have something to do with the fact that she was blushing. Her mind worked furiously. Ah. That was it. Embarrassment!

'Er,' said Onyx, for the first time in her life, and put her hand down.

'No, no,' cooed Dr Cosm evilly. 'It is good to want to help, even though some people might think you wanted to, sss, *show off*. Well, we will put you somewhere you can show off as much as you like. PREFECTS PREFECTS!'

And before Onyx knew where she was, she was in a small stone room with no windows, gazing at a pottery jug of water and Rosetti and Owen sitting on opposite sides of a table scowling at a chess set. 'Where did you get *that*?' she said.

'Owen made it,' said Rosetti. 'Out of bread.'

'Chewed bread,' said Owen.

'Uk,' said Onyx. 'Look, you can take his queen.'

'Shut *up*,' said Rosetti.

And Onyx thought: that is so unfair because I wanted to be a credit to the Head but now I haven't been but maybe it has all been a terrible mistake and actually everything is all right.

But she knew it wasn't.

And so the long day wore on, and became the long evening, and started to be the long night. Finally the cell door clattered and Miss Davies came in.

'Children, you have let me down,' she said.

'Unfair,' said Rosetti. 'I was merely honest.'

'And I was diligent,' said Owen.

'And I was keen,' said Onyx.

'How they hate all those things!' sighed Miss Davies. 'And how they hate the Headmaster! Let us go back to the Skolary.'

Owls hooted in the Quad, and the darkness pressed in on the candlelit corridors. In the Study there were no lamps, and only the firelight illuminated a dark, huddled form in a chair. 'Headmaster!' cried Onyx.

'Mm, yes, I suppose so,' said the Headmaster.

Rosetti lit a couple of lamps. 'We didn't do it,' he said, using the total denial technique that had led him to be hated by so many headmasters. 'We were framed. It was all a –'

'What?' said the Headmaster.

'We let you down,' said Rosetti. 'Like you said.'

'Me? Down?' said the Head, sounding dazed. 'Bless your hearts of course you didn't. I just wanted you to vow a bit of secrecy.'

'Wha,' said Rosetti, dazed himself.

'Never to reveal to any person alive half alive dead or undead what I am about to tell you.'

'We do! We do!' cried Onyx.

'You do what?'

'We were vowing, Headmaster,' said Miss Davies.

'Ah. Silly me. By, er, frog and stone, dog and bone, and, er, all that.'

32

'Yes, yes,' said the Skolars, meaning, get on with it.

The Head spread his hands and began to speak. 'Ahem,' said Rosetti after half a minute. 'I don't think we speak that language.'

'I do!' said Onyx. 'It's Hittite!'

'But the rest of you don't,' said the Head, flapping his long white hands. 'Not yet, no, no. Well. All that stuff today, disobedience, naughtiness. It didn't help, you know. So. The Cup. You must win it, or I shall lose my job, and Dr Cosm will be made Headmaster and there will be wall-to-wall Tests and life will be mere suffering for one and all.'

Miss Davies cleared her throat. 'Perhaps, Headmaster, it would be wise to start from the beginning. Like, what cup are you talking about?'

'Oh,' said the Headmaster. 'If you think so. The Greyte Cup, obviously. A trophy awarded every Founder's Day for Running, Hard Sums and Lovely Writing. If you don't win it, everyone will say this is proof that Polymathic Scholars are useless. Dr Cosm, that is, and the Security Masters, and Matron, and most of the Governors. And I will lose my job and they will make Dr Cosm Headmaster.' He buried his face in his hands.

To his great amazement, Rosetti found himself patting a headmaster on the back. 'There, there,' he said.

'Poor you,' said Onyx. 'Dr Cosm can't be that bad. There is good in everyone.'

'Not in him,' said the Head. 'Ever since he turned up at the beginning of last year he has schemed against me. First he turned the Governors against me by saying I was inefficient. Then he won their confidence by testing everyone all the time. He says, if you can't count it, it doesn't exist. And now it is clear that he wants my job, and he is so keen on the Cup that I think that one of the reasons is to get it in his hands. Though I do not understand what is so special about it. It is only a cup, after all. Alack, woe, he is a schemer, and his spies are everywhere, and he sits like an octopus at the centre of his web.'

'Spider, surely,' said Rosetti.

'Whatever. He seeks to destroy me.'

'How can we fix him?' said Rosetti.

'Why spider?' said Owen.

'Just win the Cup,' said the Head.

'We will,' said Owen.

'Easily,' said Onyx.

'Relax,' said Rosetti.

'Really?' said the Headmaster, his careworn features transformed by hope. 'Well, then, come, and I will show it to you!'

'Hooray!' shouted everyone. Which was odd, for the Skolars were by no means in the habit of cheering headmasters. But then Solomon Temple was obviously a far-better-than-normal sort of headmaster.

Or anyway much, much nicer than awful Dr Cosm.

Dr Cosm's room in the Duggan Cube looked like the control cabin of an executive spacecraft. One wall was entirely covered in Certificates of Toil. Another was a window looking down on a maths class battering away at hard sums.

Dr Cosm's curranty eyes swept the third wall, which was entirely covered in CCTV screens linked to the cameras that poked their little wheezing lenses into almost every corner of the Academy. His grey tongue ran round his blubbery lips. 'Otto!' he cried.

'Yes, Herr Doktor,' said the tiny Control Cabin Assistant, peering at a console through glasses like bottle-bottoms.

'Bring in number twenty-five!' snapped the Doctor.

'*Ja*, Herr Doktor! Initiating sequence! Preparing Plasma Generator! Engaging –'

'Just do it!' barked the Doctor.

The fourth wall of the room became a gigantic screen. The Skolars walked across it in line ahead, Miss Davies bringing up the rear. 'Sss,' said Dr Cosm through his smelly brown teeth. '*What* a surprise you are going to get, nyahaha.'

'Nyahaha,' said Otto.

'Shut up,' said Dr Cosm.

The Head led the way into a maze of staircases. The earlier stairs were wood, the later ones stone. From time to time little windows showed tiny pupils toiling across games pitches far below.

Finally, they arrived at a stone wall on which was carved a coat of arms topped with a monk's head holding a knife in its teeth. 'Abbot Dagger,' said Miss Davies.

'An abbot!' cried Onyx. 'And a dagger!'

'How clever,' said Rosetti politely.

'Why not a spider?' said Owen.

'Mm,' said the Head, apparently to himself. 'Dagger out of teeth, stuff up monk's right nostril, half a turn . . . ah. Mouth falls open. Grasp tongue, move it to the right.' The wall moved back with a grinding noise. 'There,' said the Head. 'The way I did that was secret. Oh. What language was I speaking?'

'English.'

'Bother. Ah, well. As I was saying, lo, the portal to the chamber of the Greyte Cup.' He waved a hand at the ancient door revealed by the moving of the wall.

'Can I open it?' said Onyx, bouncing again. 'Please? Me? Please? Me? Please? Me?' She grasped the door handle in both hands and shoved. A draught swirled through, raising a cloud of dust that hung in the air like a fog.

'Well?' said the Head, through a sneezing fit.

'Dust,' said Owen.

'And a sort of glass case,' said Onyx.

'Nobody's been in here for ages,' said Rosetti.

'Well of course not, it's the safest place in the Academy, which is itself the safest place in the country, which is frankly why you are here,' said Miss Davies, from the middle of a coughing fit. 'So open the case and let's have the Cup; it'll need a polish. Carefully, mind.'

'Well . . .' said Rosetti.

'Wha,' said Owen.

'What they mean,' said Onyx impatiently, 'is, "what cup?"'

'The one in the glass case,' said the Head.

A new draught swirled the dust. The squarish lines of a glass case revealed themselves.

An empty glass case.

The Greyte Cup for Achievement was gone.

'Oh, well,' said Onyx brightly, 'it's not the end of the world.'

The Headmaster was still sneezing, but now appeared to be weeping at the same time. So it was Miss Davies who spoke.

'My poor dear child,' she said, 'there you are wrong. The end of the world may very well be exactly what it is.'

To: All Governors
From: Abenazar Cosm, Ph.D.
It has come to my attention that the Greyte
Cup for Achievement may be missing. Nobody
is to blame, of course, and nothing is yet
proved. And many would say that if it was
true it would not be the fault of the
Headmaster. Though the Cup was in his care.
If I was made Head, nothing of the kind
would be allowed to happen. Oh no.

To: All Governors
From: Solomon Temple, Headmaster
Missing? The Cup? Piffle. Hogwash. Codswallop.
It will be on the Cup Stand at Founder's
Day.

To: The Polymathic Skolars
From: The Headmaster
Help!

3

'What are we going to *do*?' said Onyx next morning in the Study. 'Poor Headmaster!'

'We'll find it,' said Owen.

'Then win it,' said Rosetti.

'Goodee!' cried Onyx, bouncing.

'But how?' said Owen.

'We'll have a Club!' cried Onyx. 'The Pink Kitten Cup-finding Club! We'll ask all our friends –'

'Pardon me while I puke,' said Rosetti. 'No clubs. We will use the skills that got us here in the first place.'

'Being really excited!' cried Onyx. 'And reading everything!'

'Thinking about things and then doing them,' said Owen.

'Being keen on sabotage,' said Rosetti. 'And rather devious.'

'What does devious mean?'

'Being totally straightforward at all times,' said Rosetti, with a very insincere smile.

'No it doesn't!' cried Onyx.

'Exactly,' said Rosetti. He was gazing out of the window. A figure caught his eye, small and upright: the figure of their form teacher. She marched down the Cloister and opened a door. As she passed through it she looked around quickly, as if (Rosetti thought) she was checking she was not being followed. 'There's Miss Davies!' he said. 'We must tell her what we've decided and see if she's got any suggestions about how to do it. Come on!'

The Skolars ran downstairs and through the third door in the Cloister. In the distance, Miss Davies was walking across a bed of cabbages towards a tumbledown barnyard. 'After her!' said Rosetti.

They tiptoed into the barnyard in time to see Miss Davies open the door of a small round building with a cone-shaped roof. She propped the door open and walked away, as if she was going to fetch something.

'Come on!' said Rosetti. 'We'll get in there and surprise her. She'll be really impressed.'

'Hee hee,' said Onyx.

It was dark inside the building, except for a shaft of light from a hole in the middle of the roof. The air was smelly, and full of a low, happy cooing.

'It's a dovecote,' said Onyx.

'A wha?' said Owen.

'A house for keeping pigeons in.'

'Ssh!' said Rosetti.

For Miss Davies's footsteps were coming back across the yard. Rosetti suddenly had the strong feeling that she was not going to be impressed at all and that they were in the wrong place at the wrong time.

'Quick!' he said. 'Hide!'

'Why?' said Onyx.

'Where?' said Owen.

'Just hide!'

A peculiar object stood in the middle of the dovecote floor. It seemed to be a vast and ancient armchair, elaborately decorated with carvings of clocks, arrows and hourglasses, mounted on a box.

'In the box!' hissed Onyx.

In they dived.

It was dark and smelly in the box, but there was plenty of room for three. The footsteps came across the floor. The flap on the box lifted, and the Skolars braced themselves for discovery. But instead of the beautiful face of their form teacher, what appeared in the box was a basket the size and shape of a large picnic hamper. The flap closed. Above their heads the chair creaked, as if someone had climbed into it and sat down. Then a pole came down through a hole in the top of the box and began to bang up and down on the picnic hamper. From the picnic hamper there came squawks and flappings. The world became huge and dark and full of wings. Then the flapping stopped, and the chair was creaking as someone climbed off it, and the dovecote door slammed.

'Funny,' said Owen. 'I thought we went somewhere. But we're still here.'

'Me too,' said Onyx. 'Somewhere that smelled like dove muck but it was like dove muck was the nicest smell in the whole world.'

'It is,' said Rosetti in a faraway voice. 'To homing pigeons.'

'Wha.'

'So what happened?' said Onyx.

Rosetti pushed open the box. The Skolars crawled out. Things felt . . . *different*. Rosetti went and opened the dovecote door – only a crack at first to see if the coast was clear, then all the way. The Skolars stepped out of the door.

And stopped.

The world had changed.

Ten minutes ago, the farmyard had been floored with piles of rusty iron and clumps of nettles. Now it was neatly cobbled, with a pond in one corner. The tumbledown barn was not tumbledown any more. It was twice its former length and made of gleaming new oak beams with bright yellow ochre infill. There were pigsties, in which pigs grunted.

'It's so *pretty*!' cried Onyx, bouncing. 'Look at those sweet *ducks*!'

The kitchen garden had gone. In its place was

42

a rough field. Beyond the field were the Academy buildings – but changed, changed. The Duggan Cube was absent, and so was the Hall of Session. All that remained was the Tower of Flight, with next to it a big house that had a fortified look. Both the Tower and the manor house were brilliantly painted in red and yellow stripes. The sky was bright blue, far brighter than any sky the Skolars had ever seen. Against it there soared flights of doves. The doves went in and out of holes in the Tower. Rosetti watched one rise, clap its wings, glide downwards and . . .

disappear into thin air . . .

Rosetti blinked. Owen was standing on the grass, mouth open, head shaking. Onyx was bearing down on the house like a human pogo stick.

Rosetti blinked again. Then he started across the field. Owen trudged after him.

While Owen was trudging, Onyx had bounced all the way to the front door of the house, where the boys caught up. Rosetti pushed the door open and stuck his head in. There was a funny smell. Part of it might be coming from the enormous stuffed crocodile hanging up by the ceiling, and another part from the dried human hand with a candle on the end of each finger that stood on the hall table. The rest of it was dried herbs and bad drains, or perhaps no drains at all. From deep in the house came the murmur of voices.

Onyx said in a very small whisper, 'We should go back.'

'Back where?' said Rosetti.

'Wrwrwr,' said Owen. This was no place for a logical person. His eyes had crossed and would not come uncrossed.

'Noe!' cried a man's voice, huge and hollow. 'Ytt cannot bee!'

'Thou hast stole ye Cupp!' shrieked the voice of Miss Davies.

'Speak soft to thy Father,' said the hollow voice.

Father? thought Rosetti, edging closer to the room from which the voices were coming.

The man said, 'Another had done thys thyng. Fynde him!'

'Aye, we must. Or . . .'

'The Dread Thyng will come. Daughter, I yield unto thee the Doves of Time.'

('Dread thing?' hissed Onyx.

'Ssh!' hissed Rosetti.)

'Father, I thanke thee.'

'Curse!'

'Wott?'

'I have trod in my Chamber Pott!'

'Not agayne. Wait, I wyll help thee.'

There was the noise of breaking china. Onyx jumped, cannoning into Rosetti, who fell on Owen, so all the Skolars rolled down the stairs in a lump,

44

bounced off a stuffed bear and found themselves sprawled on the front doorstep.

'Run!' cried Onyx. 'They're coming!'

But Rosetti was staring at a carving in the arch above the front door: new-carved, heavily gilded, a monk's head with a dagger between its teeth. A carving so new you could see the chisel marks on it –

Onyx grabbed his hand and heaved. '*Run!*' she said.

They ran across the field, into the barnyard, into the dovecote and into the box. Five minutes later, footsteps sounded outside. The dovecote door opened. The chair creaked. The pole came down through the hole in the box lid and made its squashing movements on the hamper. Doves squawked and fluttered, the Skolars' minds filled with ideas of lovely warm nests . . .

The chair creaked. The flap opened. 'Well,' said the voice of Miss Davies. 'I think you'd all better come out now.'

The Skolars stiffened.

'I won't eat you,' said Miss Davies.

The Skolars crawled out of the box and stood in front of their teacher.

'We will go to your Study,' she said in a low, grim voice.

Oh, goodness, thought Onyx, she's *cross* and we've been *bad*! She opened her mouth to say how sorry she was and how she would never do it again ever. Then she realized that Rosetti was already speaking.

'It's all right,' he was saying. 'Your secret is safe with us, Miss Davies.' And Onyx was astonished to see a look of actual relief cross Miss Davies's face. 'As long,' said Rosetti, 'as you tell us everything.'

'Everything,' said Owen, the little robot.

'Everything,' said Onyx, trying not to faint.

'Very well,' said Miss Davies, pale, but sticking out a small, brave chin. 'Then follow me.' She marched out of the dovecote.

The world was normal again; the Duggan Cube was back, and the buildings that had been brand new during their visit to the past were once again blackened and mouldy. Miss Davies ploughed through the milling Skoolies in the Common Room and into the Polymathic Study.

The room was cold, the fire unlit. Miss Davies made a throwing gesture at it. The pile of sticks burst into flames and became a fire, warm and roaring.

'Magic!' gasped Onyx. 'You're a witch!'

Miss Davies flopped down in a chair. 'Like I told you, there is more than one explanation for everything. I flicked a match into it without your seeing. There's no such thing as magic, as in, ninky pinky hixy mixy be a toad. It is just that my father showed me how to practise hard.'

'And how to travel through time,' said Rosetti.

There was a short silence. Then Miss Davies said, 'It's not difficult. You need the right pigeons, that's all.'

'But science,' said Owen. 'Quantum mechanics. All that.'

'Tell me again. What's the motto of the Polymathic Skolars?'

'There is always more than one explanation for everything,' chorused the Skolars.

'Good. Well, it applies to Time Travel as much as everything else. There are various methods. Some end in destroying the Universe. Others are just boring. The way I use is gentle, holistic and produces very little carbon dioxide.'

'Get on with it,' said Owen, not out of rudeness but out of interest.

'It's not complicated,' said Miss Davies. 'Point one, all animals have different ideas of time. Fast to a tortoise looks slow to a hummingbird. Point two, birds that travel long distances are very good at working out where they're going. Take homing pigeons. Some people think that this is because they've got special eyes or little magnetic bits in their beaks. Well, maybe. But mostly it's because a homing pigeon has a time sense that lets it see Time backwards as well as forwards. Which means that the reason it can always find its way home is that as far as it is concerned it arrived before it left. Clear?'

Onyx said, 'Er . . .'

'Think about it,' said Miss Davies. 'Point three, flock instinct keeps birds together. Once Abbot Dagger had discovered this, the rest was easy.'

Owen said, 'Wha . . .'

'Hush. He selected pigeons from all eras, with powerful flock instinct and powerful homing instinct. The flock instinct is a sort of mind-reading that keeps a group together over long distances, even in the dark. He and his assistant, Trym, bred them, first in the dovecote, then in the Tower of Flight. Selective breeding, to make the instincts more powerful. A really powerful flock instinct affects humans too. When you were in the box you found yourselves thinking about nests, am I right? And you probably saw pigeons vanishing into thin air around the Tower. Well, they were flying around in Time.'

'But –' said Rosetti.

'Later,' said Miss Davies. 'And the flock instinct plus the homing instinct strengthened by selective breeding makes the pigeons go exactly where we want in Time, and take us with them. But there are problems. Can you think of one?'

'Paradoxes,' said Owen.

'*Caramba!*' cried Miss Davies. 'Bingo! Genius! Yes! Tell me a paradox, someone!'

Owen said, 'If someone had killed my great-grandfather, I would not be here. So if you go back in Time to kill him, I vanish. But the things I did today have already happened.'

'Excellent example!' cried Miss Davies. 'Think of Time as a river flowing from the past into the future. A small disturbance in the current makes a little eddy, which disappears. So if you eat a little slice of bread in the Middle Ages, it doesn't matter. But if you steal, say, a royal crown in the Middle Ages and bring it back to the present, you've got one stream of Time in which the crown exists and is important, and another in which it doesn't and isn't. Some silly old scientists say you can have parallel Universes, but they're wrong. A person or a thing can't exist in two Time streams at once. A paradox can only exist by stretching Time. But Time is one of those basic unstretchable universal things, like atoms. If you break up an atom, you get a huge release of energy. If you split a Time stream, you get something worse: a release of historical energy called a Dread Thing, when History more or less blows up and starts again.'

There was a silence. Then a hand went up. Obviously, it was Onyx's.

'Miss miss please miss,' she said.

'Yes, Onyx?'

'How do you know all this?'

Miss Davies gave her a charming smile. 'Because,' she said, 'Abbot Dagger is my father, and I keep an eye on things for him in future Time. I talk to him across Time, when he is listening. It's a knack.'

'Oh,' said Onyx, and thought for a bit.

Owen had no time for all this vague stuff. He said, 'What has this got to do with the Greyte Cup being stolen?'

'Much better question than usual,' said Miss Davies. 'Ideas, anyone? Given that the Greyte Cup has been stolen from a locked room that no one has visited since last year?'

'Tell us,' said Rosetti.

'Well,' said Miss Davies, 'if you wanted to hide something, where would you put it?'

'In a hole,' said Owen.

'Or?'

'In a cupboard,' said Onyx.

'Or?'

'Somewhere else in Time,' said Rosetti.

'Correct, said Miss Davies. 'Well done. I've got a feeling that this is where we should look first.'

'Feeling?' said Owen, who did not understand the term.

'Hunch.'

'Oh,' said Owen, still baffled.

There was a short but very deep silence. Then Onyx put her hand up so hard that all her bones cracked.

'Onyx?' said Miss Davies.

'So all we've got to do,' said Onyx, 'is get some

50

pigeons and go back and find the Cup in Time and bring it back for Founder's Day or the Headmaster will lose his job and Dr Cosm will become Headmaster and make the Skool even worse than it already is and the world may end because of a Dread Thing happening. And it's only four and a half weeks till Founder's Day so we'd better get going.'

'Spot on,' said Miss Davies. 'We've already got the pigeons.'

'Hooray!' said Onyx. 'Come on, everyone!'

Five days later, on Monday of the following week, at the end of a Lovely Writing lesson, Miss Davies clapped her hands. 'Dismiss!' she cried. Then, over the thunder of boots on floorboards, 'Polymathic Skolars, to me!' She waited till the rest of the class had left the room. 'Now!' she cried. 'Great news! We're off! Wear games kit! Meet at the dovecote after lunch!'

But it was not as easy as that. For after lunch the Prefects herded the pupils into the Hall of Session, where Nurse Drax and Corporal Prang were standing on the stage.

'Cleanliness Test!' bawled a great voice.

'But we have to go back to –' said Onyx.

'Oh, no,' snarled a voice from on high. She looked up. Far above her, Slee Duggan grinned evilly. 'There is no going back.'

'Y-yes, sir,' said Onyx.

Slee bent towards her. 'Good luck,' he said, and she felt something wipe her legs.

'Th-thanks,' she said. Looking down, she saw her knees had turned black.

'Pork-fat soot,' said Slee. 'Hyeugh hyeugh.'

'Hyeugh hyeugh,' said Elphine the Match Girl admiringly.

Oo, you creep! thought Onyx.

Ahead, pupils were stepping on to the dais, where Nurse Drax was examining their faces and knees with a cracked magnifying glass. Ooer, thought Onyx, scrubbing at her knee with her sleeve. Her sleeve got filthy and her knees got no cleaner. Then she was going up the steps, and Nurse Drax's breath was all around her like a sickly fog. And an awful silence fell.

'Look at you!' hissed the voice. 'Look at the *state* of you!' Onyx's eyes began to prickle. 'You will learn not to trifle with the Cleanliness Tests!' hissed the voice. 'And the way you will learn it is to write a thousand times "I must be more cleanerer".'

'Do you mean "cleaner"?'

'No good trying to make 'em shorter! Write two thousand!'

Onyx said in a tiny voice, 'Yes, Mato,' and shuffled out of the breath fog.

'Next reptile!' snarled Matron.

The next reptile was actually Owen, whose

hyper-logical mind could not tolerate anything random like dirt. So he passed the test and went on to Corporal Prang.

''Shun!' cried a Security Master.

Owen sprang to attention.

'March!' cried a Security Master.

Owen began to march.

Rosetti approached the steps of the dais. As he raised his foot for the first step, Damage Duggan pushed him from behind, causing him to trip over the bottom step and bash his knee quite severely.

'Hyeugh hyeugh,' said Damage.

Rosetti tried not to be angry. But he did not quite succeed, and the anger touched another mind, a small, hot mind, sloshing with blood; the mind of the woewolf he had befriended. Woewolves have special talents, chief of which is coming when called and vanishing when not needed. In a split second a green-toothed grey creature had materialized at the foot of the steps and leaped at Flanker Duggan's throat –

Ooer, thought Rosetti. Begone, woewolf.

The teeth clashed six inches under Damage's chin, and the woewolf vanished. And there was Rosetti limping past the black-clad Security Masters and on to the stage, and Matron and the whole Skool staring at Damage, who was strangling the air in front of his face and howling . . .

Not actually the whole Skool. Three people were

53

not looking. One of them was Owen, because he was marching and nobody had told him to stop. Another was Onyx, because she had got tangled up with Owen and was being marched herself. And the other was Rosetti, because he had noticed the narrow but useful hole in the crowd made by his fellow Skolars, and was pounding down it as fast as he could go. He overtook Owen just as he was about to crash into the wall.

'Right turn!' he hissed, running ahead to open the door. 'Left turn! Halt! Act normal!'

'What do you mean, normal?' said Owen.

'I've got all these *lines*!' wailed Onyx, with the true grief of the affronted keenie.

'Never mind the lines,' said Rosetti. 'Run! To the Study!'

They ran.

Miss Davies was sitting with her feet on the desk painting a fingernail. 'Where have you *been*?' she said.

They told her, panting. 'And,' said Rosetti, 'I'm afraid we've let the Headmaster down again.'

'And I've got all these *lines*!' wailed Onyx.

'Relax,' said Miss Davies. 'My father employs demons who write millions in seconds. Let's go!'

Five minutes later, Dr Cosm and a squad of Security Masters arrived outside the Study door.

'Open up,' cried Cosm. Silence.

'Break the door down.'

Four hefty Security Masters hurled themselves at the door. They fell back cursing and rubbing bumps, for it was stout and ancient and studded with nails.

'Sss!' cried Cosm, striding to the front. 'What is that?'

A Security Master squinted at the white rectangle pinned to the door. 'A Nonvelope,' he said, tearing it off.

'Addressed to the Headmaster,' said Cosm. 'I'll open it.'

'Actually I think I will,' said an even, jolly voice, approaching from the end of the corridor. 'Being the Headmaster, and all that.'

'For the moment only, sss,' muttered Cosm.

The Head smiled sweetly and opened the envelope. 'Oh, look. They have gone on a field trip. How very acceptable!'

'Having caused mayhem and chaos at a Skool Cleanliness Test and disrupted the education of their fellow pupils,' said Cosm. 'Let us explain these shocking events to the Governors. How fortunate that there is a meeting in an hour!'

'Item six,' said Dr Cosm, whose turn it was to run the Governors' Meeting. 'Behaviour of this year's new Polymathic Skolars. Very bad.'

'In what way?' said Colonel De'ath, who liked to get to the bottom of things.

'Lack of cleanliness.'

'All our pupils are filthy,' said the Headmaster, beaming.

'Not as filthy as your Polymathics. Plus there was lack of respect while marching.'

'Tut!' said Police Commissioner Bruce Manacle between clenched teeth.

'Summoning of wild animals contrary to school rules thereby endangering staff health and safety.'

'But aren't the other pupils just as bad?' said Inkon Stimp R.A. the artist.

'Who asked you?' cried Lady Squee.

'Not the point!' cried Professor Tube.

'The Polymathics are the Head's personal responsibility. So I propose that the Headmaster be sacked instantly,' said Cosm with ghastly eagerness.

'Sounds fine to –'

'Ahem,' said the Headmaster. 'I fear that this is not allowed. The ancient statutes of the Abbot say, not in the middle of a term, no way, José. May I suggest that we give the Skolars time to settle in? And, as the Colonel proposed at our last meeting, to win the Greyte Cup for Achievement? In Running, Colonel. And Hard Sums, Professor. And Lovely Writing, Mr Stimp. Well?'

'So we can't sack you?' said Cosm.

'Absolutely not.'

'Hah!' said Cosm. 'Well, a statute is a statute, I

suppose, and all reasonable people know that the law is the law, yes, sss. But there are only three point seven two eight five one weeks till Founder's Day. For now, I suggest that the Colonel declare this meeting closed.' He stacked his papers. 'Sss, start packing, Head,' he muttered under his breath. 'No one will stand in my way. Next term, the Skool. Afterwards, the Universe.'

'What?' said the Colonel.

'Nothing,' said Cosm.

4

In the dovecote the Skolars were settling into the Time Chair and Miss Davies was stuffing the Time Doves into the basket. 'Ready?'

'Aye.'

She prodded the basket with her pole. Squawk, flap, thoughts of nests. Then they were back in the reign of Elizabeth I, walking across the new-old farmyard and into the brightly painted house by the Tower. It was nice to have a guide.

'Hand of Glory,' said Miss Davies, pointing at the human hand with the candles on it. 'And this,' she said, pausing opposite a sausage-like object wrapped in dirty bandages and propped against a wall, 'is a speaking mummy, certified Ancient Egyptian. Go on, talk to it.'

'What's your name?' said Onyx.

'Can't remember, silly me,' said the mummy in a hoarse, dry voice.

'It's called Pft,' said Miss Davies. 'None too bright when he was alive, let alone after he had died and someone had pulled his brains out of his nose with a little hook.' The sound of a splosh and swearing came from above. 'There's Dad,' she said. 'Stepped in his chamber pot again.' She shooed her pupils up the stairs and into a large, smelly room. A man was sitting in a carved chair by the fire. He was wearing a floor-length black robe embroidered with mystic sigils. Under the robe, he seemed to be trying to shake something off his foot.

'Sdeath,' he roared. 'Oh. Greetyngs, faire daughter.' He rose, checking that his robe covered the foot. 'And these wyll be thy Skolars.' He burst into a flow of gibberish. Onyx stepped forward, made a courteous sign with her hand, and spoke back to him. He looked very surprised. 'Thou speakest Hittite!' he cried.

'I get by,' said Onyx.

'Verilie, thys ys a marvell,' said Abbot Dagger, stepping back. There was the sound of breaking china. The smell grew stronger. 'Argh! Trym!' he bawled. 'Ye Mopp!'

'Oh, no, not agayne!' said a voice below, thin and cross.

'Perhaps we will take a look around the house,' said Miss Davies hastily.

'Sounde Scheeme,' said the Abbot.

For half an hour the children examined jewels, eggs and Marvels of Art. When they returned to the Abbot's chamber, the sage was seated in his chair with his feet in a basket of sweet herbs. A man shuffled out of the room, clanking a mop and bucket. He looked rather angry and rather odd, because of the eye tattooed in the middle of his forehead. 'I be Trym,' he said. 'Keeper of the Doves, tattooed with the Alle-Seeing Eye. Withoute whome thys whole place would falle to byts –'

'Silence, showoff. Thyne eye is mere decoration and thy head is huge,' said the Abbot.

'Father,' said Miss Davies, 'we crave a boon. We crave that thou wylt tell us the true and amazing Historie of the Greyte Cupp. Begge Hymme,' she hissed to the children behind her hand.

'It would be an honour,' said Rosetti.

'Just tell it to us and cut the cackle,' said Owen.

'Please!' said Onyx, bouncing. 'Please please please please –'

'Verily thou arte keene,' said the Abbot, wrinkling his nose. 'Well, heere goes. Ye Cupp ys mine. But I hyd ytt, for thys reason. I herde from Fryends at Courte that Her Majestie planned to send Leeches and Bloodsuckers upon me, to counte my Riches and take the half portion of them as Taxes, sayynge, One who hath the Skill Necromantick can always make more. Whych is not Right, the Thieves. Soe I took Measures. Soe that when the Leeches came, pox on them and most of all on Abanazer their Cheefe, theye found mee in a three-legged chayre under a roofe with holes in, and alle my flocks, herds, jewels, eggs and Marvells of Arte hidden where they could not be founde. And the Greyte Cupp I hyd not in place, with all my other goodes, but in Forward Tyme against the cunning of this Abanazar. And nowe ytt has gone, I hear. Soe ye must go toe a place yn Tyme where ye Cupp exysteth yet, and take ytt, and place ytt once more in ye Sealed Roome. If ytt bee kept hydden from mortal eye in ye Roome, all wyll be well, for ytt wyll have no effect on Events, being locked away. But if ytt be out in the World, and mayhap cause Tyme to Divide, then may come to pass the Dread Thyng.'

'My head hurts,' said Rosetti.

'Simple,' said Owen. 'We go back into the past, steal the Cup before it was stolen and put it back in the Sealed Room after it was stolen.'

'But then it wouldn't be there to be owned by Abbot Dagger and hidden in the future.'

'Yes it would,' said Owen. 'Because what has happened has already happened, or there would never have been a Cup at the Skool.'

'My head,' said Rosetti.

'Children,' said Miss Davies, 'we will all go mad if we argue about this. What we must do first is go back in Time, find the Cup and put it in the Sealed Room.'

'Have a care,' said the Abbot. 'Beware that ye

cause not a Dread Thyng. Daughter, hast thou looked in the Indispensible Examinator?'

'Noe.'

'Go forthe,' said the Abbot.

As they left the room, he was pouring perfume on his foot.

They entered a distant part of the house. Miss Davies pulled a lever. A door opened. They walked down a passage whose walls began to shake. The reason for the shaking, it turned out, was a stone gully full of huge water wheels that ran beside the passage. Miss Davies shooed them through this, and into a room full of the glitter of light.

'The Examinator,' she said. 'We use it for looking through Time.'

'How does it work?' said Owen.

'Very badly,' said Miss Davies. 'It is done with mirrors.' She began to haul a series of levers of the kind found in old-fashioned railway signal boxes. 'And it is very inaccurate. What I am doing now is programming. With luck we will soon see a picture of what the Academy will look like if the Greyte Cup is still missing on Founder's Day. Look at that wall over there.'

The wall was covered with glittering little motes of light. Gradually the motes came together. A picture started to form.

'That's not the Academy,' said Onyx.

Rosetti was silent.

The mountains beyond the Rim looked the same. But where the Academy buildings should have been was a sheet of brown water. Something disturbed the surface. A long green neck came up. At the end of the neck was a reptile head full of fierce teeth.

'Wha,' said everybody.

'Remember what I said about the River of Time,' said Miss Davies. 'A small eddy in Time disappears, so if you eat a little slice of bread in the Middle Ages it doesn't matter. But if you nick a crown, someone is going to notice, and you change the course of the river, and there will be trouble. In this case, the Examinator is showing what will happen if we do not find the Cup and put it back in the Sealed Room. The very fabric of Reality has been torn, and the dinosaurs will still be ruling the Earth, and most of the Universe will be different too. To sum up: if the Cup doesn't get back in time for prizegiving on Founder's Day, there will be bigger problems than the Head losing his job and Cosm taking over. The Skool will never have existed. And nor will we.'

'In that case,' said Rosetti, 'we'd obviously better go and find the Cup. But where do we start?'

'Ask the Examinator!' cried Onyx.

'Not sensitive enough,' said Miss Davies. There was a crash and a rumble and the slipping roar of falling masonry. 'And very badly built. That's it fallen down. We'll ask Papa.'

Back they trooped to the Abbot's room, where the smell was now absolutely ghastly and Trym was skulking with a bucket.

'Father,' said Miss Davies, through her hanky. 'I abjure you by all Demons and Laws to tell us, where should we start our Quest?'

'Hence, Trym, vermin, begone,' said the Abbot. Trym shot him a nasty look and clanked off. The Abbot frowned. His eyes rolled back in his head and he crashed back into his chair in a trance. '*Alboolah blimpast skweedragora*,' he said.

'Language?' said Miss Davies.

Onyx frowned. 'Sort of pidgin Assyrian with hints of Ancient Egyptian. Nonsense really.'

'Just as I thought,' said Miss Davies. 'Pater, how did you come by that Cup?'

The Abbot came round swiftly. 'Someone . . . gave it unto mee.'

'Oh, yeah,' said his daughter disrespectfully. 'You nicked it, didn't you?'

'Alack,' said the Abbot, looking shifty. 'I remember mee nott how –'

'You would have nicked it somewhen back in time,' said Miss Davies. 'Like you nicked the mummy off the Priest Tot.'

'Fie!'

'Mayhap I wyll place ye contents of yon other dysgustynge Chamber Pott on thy scurvy Hedde,' said Miss Davies.

'Noe! Groo! I confesse! Ytt was yn ye hands of ye Knights Templar that darkest of Fryedays. I took ytt then!'

'Then we will go back and find it ourselves, before you do, and put it in the Sealed Room,' said Miss Davies. 'I shall get a supply of Doves from Trym. Come, Skolars.'

'My lines!' said Onyx. 'What about my lines?'

'Ah yes. Father, two thousand times I Must be More Cleanerer.'

'I wyll telle the Demons and Trym will send them by Dove, the knave. Now begone!'

Miss Davies talked to Trym, who could be heard whining and complaining.

The Skolars ran to the dovecote. In went the dove basket. Down went the pole. And there was the dirty old Skool farmyard again.

Phew.

Four days later, tea was ready in the Study in the Skolary. A large pan of sausages (sent down by the Head, who thought the Skool food was disgusting) was cooking on the open fire. Beside it, a teapot steamed on a trivet. Beside the fire sat Onyx, a leather-bound book open on her knee and a crumpet in her hand. As Rosetti and Owen walked in, slightly stained with mud from Running practice, they noticed she was bouncing.

'This is amazing!' she said. 'I found it in the

Library. In 1307 the King of France wanted to get rid of the Templars who were sort of monk knights because they were too powerful and he wanted their treasure so he sent the army into their headquarters in Paris and looted it and burned it and put the head Templar in prison but the head Templar cursed him and from that day on the kings of France were absolutely useless and Miss Davies says we can go and see them on the actual day they were raided i.e. Black Friday the thirteenth of October 1307!'

'Oh,' said Rosetti, panting slightly.

'Wha,' said Owen.

'Like the Abbot said,' said Onyx. 'The Temple. In Paris. The darkest of Fryedays, he called it. This is it!'

Miss Davies came in. 'Wash, tea and dovecote!' she said briskly. 'And we'll get the Cup, and come home. It'll be hard on the doves, of course.'

'Why?' said Rosetti.

'Normally they take about five days to recharge. But this lot haven't been used much lately, so we should be all right.'

Half an hour later they were at the dovecote, full of tea.

Miss Davies got everyone settled on the Time Chair. 'Now, then, children, I want you to behave,' she said. 'Where we are going you may find people are a little . . . on edge.' She consulted a large leather-bound book and a stop-watch. 'Two. One.

Go!' she cried, mashing the pole on to the dove basket. There was the squawk, the flutter, the feeling of warm nests in the mind. 'Here we are,' said Miss Davies. 'I shall remain with the doves and defend the Cote. You will be novices, which means trainee monks. You will find the Cup, nick it and bring it back here. Be careful.' She rummaged in a basket and pulled out some robes. 'Put these on. Onyx has done the —'

'Research!' cried Onyx, bouncing. 'I have! I have! We are to consign ourselves to the care and teaching of Father Anselm, the Novice Master, who will definitely show us around because he needs new novices. It'll be just like being first-day-at-Skool again! And then we'll take the Cup! How thrrrrilling!'

'Go,' said Miss Davies.

The robes were long and black, with hoods. The Skolars ducked into them, then pushed open the dovecote door.

They were standing on a green lawn. There was a brown pond on which ducks were floating. Around the lawn was a high grey wall, pierced by a mighty gateway blocked with a portcullis and an iron-bound gate. From the gate a cobbled path led across the lawn to a castle. The path was crowded with people and horses. The people looked small, the horses hairy. There was the smell of History again: sweat and no drains.

'Hoods up,' said Rosetti. 'Quick march. Let's get that Cup and get back here and get out as fast as possible.' He bowed his head and moved towards the castle gate with a smooth, gliding step. The other two Skolars glided after him.

The smell increased as the crowd thickened. Two surly-looking guards stood at the castle gate, pikes crossed. Onyx pushed forward. '*Novitiae sumus,*' she cried in fluent Latin. '*Ingressare volimus!*'

'Oo,' said the guards, uncrossing their pikes. The Skolars marched in, and found themselves in a little room with sawdust on the floor and two hard benches. Magazines had not yet been invented, but even so they recognized it as a waiting room.

Five minutes later the door crashed open. There was a smell of stale wine and a flutter of robes. A man was standing in front of them.

'Hic,' he said.

Gibber, gibber, went Onyx.

Gibber, gibber, hic, replied the winey man.

'This is Anselmus the Novice Master, as I hoped,' said Onyx. 'I have told him we are very eager to maybe join the Templars and would like to be shown around. He says there have not been any novices for ages and we must be crazy, but fine.'

'Ahee!' cried the Novice Master, and zigzagged off down a stone passage.

'Follow him!' cried Onyx.

'*Cappella!*' cried Anselm, throwing open a door.

'The chapel!' translated Onyx.

'Ooer!' cried Rosetti.

They stood for a moment under the barrel-vault of a huge church, their eyes swimming with incense and dazzled by the glitter of jewels on images. There was no Cup that they could see. Then they were off again. They wove through long tables crowded with warrior monks eating steaks off the points of their daggers. Still no Cup.

Then Anselmus was zigzagging again, past bedrooms and a long smelly room with a lot of holes in a stone slab –

'Smell like lavs,' said Owen.

'Actually they are *reredorters*.'

'Smell like lavs.'

'That is because lavs are exactly what they are. Interestingly enough –'

Rosetti hissed, 'We need the Cup. Which means we need to be taken to the treasure chamber. And in a hurry.'

'But I was *explaining*!' said Onyx.

'Explain later.'

'Tch,' said Onyx, and asked for the Thesaurus, which was 'treasure chamber' in Latin. Anselmus led the way through three thick doors guarded by nasty-looking armed men.

'I can hear something,' said Rosetti.

'Me too,' said Owen.

'No. Inside my head. A Call.'

'Duh,' said Owen.

'I think it's the Cup.'

Anselmus led them into a dark room. He said, '*Ecce!*'

'Behold,' translated Onyx.

'Ulp,' said Owen.

They were standing on the floor of a tower. A single ray of sun lanced from a high window on to an arrangement of chests and shelves in the centre of the circular room. The light blazed on gold and silver. It struck diamonds and rubies and emeralds, and burst into thousands of new colours that shot on to the dark walls and lay twinkling like a new universe in a black sky. And there on the right, on a stand of its own, was a gold cup, the knop halfway down its stem studded with big red stones.

'The Greyte Cup!' said Onyx.

'Told you,' said Rosetti. 'It was Calling.'

'Never mind that,' said Owen. 'Let's have it.'

'But how will you get it out?' said Rosetti.

'Stun the guards. Run.'

Rosetti looked at the guards, who were large and heavily armed. He said, 'They will stun us first.'

The Novice Master was talking.

'He says this is all really, *really* ancient stuff,' said Onyx, bouncing slightly. 'He says that thing is the Prophet Elijah's thumb in a box of richest work.

And he says that cup over there is actually the Holy Grail, which came from the vaults of the Cathedral that Burned. I told him it's an important Skool Prize but I don't think he heard.'

'The Holy what?' said Rosetti.

Owen took a step towards the Cup. Five big guards took a step towards Owen. Rosetti said, 'Perhaps we'd better have a little think about this.'

At this point, there was a sort of thickening of the air. The thickening became a solidity, and took the form of a chair sitting on a closed basket. A lanky figure was sitting on the chair. The air was filled with the cooing of doves.

The figure on the chair got up. His robe was covered with moons and stars and Sigils of Art.

'Abbot Dagger!' cried Onyx.

The Abbot did not seem to be listening. He got off his chair, scooped up the Greyte Cup, stowed it in his robes and returned to the chair, knocking over the Thumb of Elijah.

There were cries of fury. Jewels skittered across the stone floor. The figure on the chair said something that sounded like, 'Ooer,' and kicked the basket under the seat. Doves squawked. The figure began to fade. Armed men advanced on him from all sides, spears and axes raised.

A huge bell started to ring. A din of metal came from outside, and a confused roaring of voices.

'Whoops,' said Rosetti, who had heard trouble before.

'They are saying that the troops of Philippe le Bel are storming the outer walls,' said Onyx. 'He's the king, by the way. Correction, *have* stormed.' Arrows clattered on the ceiling. 'Perhaps we should, ooer, come back later.'

'Quite,' said Rosetti. 'Thank you, gents,' he said to the guards. He led the Skolars swiftly past the Novice Master and out of the Thesaurus.

The stone corridors were full of people. 'To the battlements!' yelled Rosetti, and led his fellow Skolars down the steps to the duck-pond lawn. Even here the air was full of arrows. People were milling and howling. Several things seemed to be on fire, and a huge battering noise came from the gates. Onyx was looking rather white. The crowd moved aside, and there was the dovecote, with Miss Davies at the door.

'Quick!' cried Miss Davies. In they ran.

The door slammed. There was an explosion outside, the sound of the gate bursting inwards, the skitter of arrows on the dovecote roof. Miss Davies stamped on the dove basket. Rosetti said, 'Ow!'

'What is it?'

'A stone. It's freezing cold.'

'Where is it?'

'Pocket.' He rummaged in his pocket and pulled out a stone that glittered.

'Where did you get that?'

'Treasure-room floor.'

The dovecote door burst open. An archer stood there, bow bent, arrow pointing straight at Miss Davies.

Miss Davies gave the archer her dazzling smile. She took the jewel out of Rosetti's hand and tossed it to him. 'Catch,' she said.

The jewel looped through the air, twinkling like a tiny sun, and fell to the earth. Already halfway to his knees to pick up the jewel, the archer loosed his arrow. It thunked into the woodwork of the chair. Miss Davies stamped on the dove basket. Nests filled the heads of all. Then they were still in the dovecote, but there was no archer, and the arrow in the chairback was crumbling into dust, and from outside came the distant comforting sound of games being played on muddy pitches. They were back at Skool.

'Skolars, and specially Rosetti,' said Miss Davies severely, 'I know that some of your parents were jewel thieves. But I tell you here and now for the very last time, nicking stuff is very, very wrong, and I have to remind you about the Examinator, which showed that nicking stuff in History will cause more trouble than you can imagine. That jewel you tried to nick went into the Crown of Britain, and its absence from the Crown would have changed things very nastily, and ended the Universe, so don't even think about doing it again.' She jumped down from the chair. 'Now come on, everyone. Debrief. Then supper. Then I want you all to write a few pages on What We Did in the Middle Ages.'

They went to the Study, where a warm fire was blazing. 'Well?' said Miss Davies.

'Your dad nicked the Cup,' said Owen. 'We saw him do it.'

Miss Davies sighed. 'I was afraid of that,' she said. 'We're not used to Time Travel yet, and practice makes perfect, and the Abbot's had loads of practice. Anyone got any ideas about what to do next?'

Onyx's hand was already up, creaking with upness. 'Miss miss please miss I have miss please.'

'Well, Onyx?'

'The Novice Master said it came from the Vaults of the Cathedral that Burned!' said Onyx. 'So all we have to do is find out which cathedral! And then go and steal it!'

'But –' said Rosetti, frowning.

Whatever he had been going to say was drowned in the tolling of a great bell, and the thunder of thick boots on oak floors.

'Supper!' cried Miss Davies. 'Along you go, chop chop!'

As they ran, Rosetti said to Owen, 'If that little jewel didn't want to be moved in Time, what would have happened if we had got the Cup?'

74

Owen said, doggedly, 'A Dread Thing, obviously. So the Cup must be different.'

'How?'

Owen's eyes were beginning to cross. 'Not enough data.'

'And how will it be there for the Abbot to nick if we nick it from this Cathedral?'

'Same answer,' said Owen, joining the food queue. 'Now can we talk about something else because if we don't my eyes will cross again and I'll start bumping into things.'

After supper Onyx made her way to the library.

The Academy Library occupied several floors of the Tower of Flight – it was hard to say exactly how many because of the deep drifts of dust that covered many of its shelves and staircases. Onyx borrowed a wheelbarrow from the Librarian, piled it full of books and wheeled it to a table by a window. She began to open books, leaf through and slam them on a pile. The Librarian opened his mouth to tell her to be gentle. Dust drifted in. He felt one of his asthma attacks coming on. Wrapping a wet handkerchief round his face he went back to his game of patience, trying to ignore the sneezing coming from the middle of the dust cloud.

'*Choo*,' it went. *Slam* went another book.

'*Choo*.' *Slam*.

'Choo. *Reeka!*'

A small figure lurched out of the dust cloud carrying an enormous volume.

'I'm borrowing this book,' said Onyx, and shot out of the Library. The Librarian pressed a button on his communicator. 'Dr Cosm?' he wheezed.

'What?' barked the lard-white Doctor.

'Librarian here.'

'What have I got to do with books? I hate books,' snarled Cosm. 'Can you test them? Can you count their contents? No!'

'I admire you greatly,' wheezed the Librarian. 'Just as I admire all Great Men who will one day become Headmasters. And I thought you would like to know that one of the Targets is reading up on Chartres Cathedral.'

'Oh,' said Cosm. 'Yes. Quite. When the Great Day comes you will not regret this, worm.'

'Oo, ta,' wheezed the Librarian.

Next morning, the Skolars fought their way through the Skoolie crowds back to the Study. Miss Davies was standing before an easel, over which she had laid a red velvet cloth. 'I would like to show you an excellent bit of research by Onyx,' she said. 'It concerns something she has found out about Chartres Cathedral, in France. Behold.' She swept off the red cloth.

'How very beautiful,' said Rosetti.

On the easel was a large book, open at an

illustration of a stained-glass window. It was indeed a beautiful window, bearing a picture of a tall tree with smaller pictures growing from its branches. The glass was richly coloured in blues and crimsons and deep viridian greens.

And golds.

'On the right-hand side, three panels from the top,' said Miss Davies. 'What do you see?'

'A cup,' said Owen. 'Made of gold. With red stones on the knop.'

'The Greyte Cup,' said Rosetti. 'Obviously. But why would anyone put the Greyte Cup in a stained-glass window?'

'Beautiful thing,' said Miss Davies. 'Ancient.'

Rosetti looked at her closely. Unless he was much mistaken, she was hiding something. He remembered what the Templar Novice Master had said. 'And apparently,' he said, 'it is the Holy Grail.'

Miss Davies laughed. 'When you've knocked about in Time as much as I have, you'll find that just about every tea mug is apparently the Holy Grail.'

'Oh,' said Rosetti. But –'

'Anyway,' said Miss Davies, cutting him off, 'the doves will be ready in five days. At which point we will go back and nick the Cup from Chartres Cathedral. Till then this is a Skool. And there is no point in bringing the Cup back unless we're going to win it once it's here. It is exactly three weeks till Founder's Day. So, Onyx, do lots of Lovely Writing. And, Owen, keep in practice with those Hard Sums. And, Rosetti, run as you have never run before. And the Polymathic Skolars will triumph, and Cosm will be defeated, and our dear Headmaster will be able to keep his job, and revolting Cosm will not get his hands on our dear Skool.'

'But it's not our dear Skool,' said Owen, with crushing logic. 'We're here because we're impossible.'

'We could make it lovelier,' said Onyx keenly.

'How?'

'Paint it pink? Or palest blue,' said Onyx, remembering that there were boys present.

'Or scupper Cosm,' said Rosetti.

'For which we will first need the Greyte Cup,' said Miss Davies.

'Hooray!' cried the Skolars, inspired.

'Doves ready on Thursday at six. Till then, practice makes perfect!'

Four days later, high in the Observation Room of the Duggan Cube, Dr Cosm sat and gnawed his fingernails. It was all very well the Librarian telling him things. But quantum engines took time to charge up . . .

Still, there did not seem to be any hurry. The Library screens showed a cloud of dust with two pigtails sticking out of it at sharp angles. The soundtrack consisted mostly of the coughing and wheezing of the Librarian. In the silences between sneezes could be heard the scritch of a pen doing Lovely Writing. Cosm was gagging to punish someone for something, but there was absolutely nothing to punish there. Gnagn, he thought, turning to the Main Skool Screen. The sound of applause came tinnily over the loudspeakers.

'It's obvious,' said a voice. Then there was the squeak of chalk on slate. Dr Cosm zoomed in.

The camera settled on the stocky figure of Owen French. He had his back to the camera and his face to a huge blackboard. His hand was whizzing over its surface, scrawling an amazingly hard sum. He finished a line, added an equals sign and wrote 'five camels'. Sections of the room erupted into cheering.

Gnarghnsch, thought Dr Cosm. He hated geniuses, because they were impossible to Test. 'Where's Svenson?' he barked.

'Here.'

'Where?'

'Running track,' said Otto.

'Put him on.' The scene changed to green grass and grey drizzle, and a lean child running smoothly and fast, overtaking other running children. 'Hah,' said Dr Cosm. 'So there you are, my friend. But not for long. Nyahaha!'

'Nyahaha!' said Otto.

'Shut up,' said Dr Cosm.

Rosetti did not much like racing. So he had worked out that the best thing to do was run much faster than anyone else, so you did not actually notice you were in a race. Today he was hurtling around the perimeter track at eighteen miles an hour, watching a rabbit that was running away from him flat out and realizing that flat out was not going to be fast enough. But Rosetti's mind was not on rabbits. Rosetti's mind was on the Holy Grail.

'Oi!' said a voice beside him.

He looked to his left and saw Slee Duggan, riding a bicycle. 'You are pafetic,' said Slee Duggan.

'Tell you what,' said Rosetti, with a kind smile, 'your mother is a baboon.' Slee's heavy brows frowned. His little eyes crossed.

'Oi,' said a voice on Rosetti's right.

Rosetti looked to his right, and saw Damage Duggan, riding another bicycle. 'And your mother,' he said, 'was a different baboon from his mother.'

Damage's heavy brows frowned. His little eyes crossed, deep in thought. 'Oi,' said Damage. 'You dissin' our mum?'

'Yeah,' said Slee. 'He's dissin' our mum.'

The Duggans said, 'Rrrr.' Having caused trouble according to Dr Cosm's instructions, they surged towards Rosetti.

This was very much what Rosetti had been hoping for. He stopped dead and ran in the opposite direction. Instead of surging into him, the Duggans surged into each other. There was the sound of mixed crashing. When he looked back, he saw Slee's head sticking through the spokes of Damage's front wheel, and Damage's leg wrapped in Slee's chain. 'Oo dearie me,' said Rosetti. 'Oof.'

For he had collided with something large and solid: a Security Master. 'You bin spotted bullyin' them pore little big lads,' said the Security Master. 'Come wif me to the Duty Master.'

'And the Duty Master's Dr Cosm, isn't it?' said Rosetti, spotting the Security Master's earpiece. 'Hello, Doctor!' He waved.

'Gnaaah!' shrieked an insect voice in the Security Master's ear. The master tore the earpiece out and clutched his head. 'Extra Tests!' cried the earpiece. 'Report instantly to the Duggan Cube!'

Rosetti shrugged, and trotted off to the Physics laboratories. It was a silly childish skooly sort of punishment, very unfair, typical of Dr Cosm. Well, if Dr Cosm wanted to be childish and skooly, Rosetti could be childish and skooly right back.

These thoughts of revenge pushed thoughts of the Holy Grail out of his head.

For the moment.

*

Dr Cosm was delighted to have a chance to punish the brat Svenson. He sent him to sit in the White Room, and wrote a physics problem on the board. 'Nyah,' he said. 'Finish this and show your workings. I have some very important meetings to go to. Your every movement is, of course, watched.' He waved a hand at the TV camera high on the white wall.

Rosetti looked at the problem on the board, a thing containing weights, springs and electricity. It was not a very interesting problem, but it was not very difficult either. As he finished, the tea bell was tolling. Rosetti did a drawing of Cosm being eaten by a machine, and made sure the CCTV camera saw it. Then he left the answer to the problem on the desk, got his stuff together and set off. But he did not go straight to the Study.

He had an errand to do first. In the kitchens, and elsewhere. An errand of revenge on Cosm.

People said revenge was sweet.

Sweet? said Rosetti in his mind. You ain't seen nothing yet.

5

At bedtime that evening, Dr Cosm found himself rather tired. He brushed his teeth exactly six hundred times. Then he washed his large white face, vaulted into his large green pyjamas and went to bed. He had designed his bedroom himself. It had white walls and a white ceiling; Dr Cosm hated colours. The bed was white too. Its duvet was large and white and soft. Tonight, it felt extra delightful, like being covered by a cloud. As every day, Dr Cosm turned out the lights and lay for a moment running over in his mind his plans to take over the Skool. The Governors were on his side. As for the rest . . . well, things were going very well . . .

The pasty lids fell over the curranty eyes.

Dr Cosm slept.

Some time later, he woke up. He opened his eyes. It was dark. Also, it was *sticky*. He raised a hand. The duvet rose with it. He swung his feet out of bed. The duvet swung with them. He stood up in the dark. The duvet stood up too, clinging to him.

'Help!' shouted Dr Cosm, trying to wrench free. Something tore. Suddenly the air was full of feathers. 'Aiee! Noo!' he cried again. His mouth filled with feathers. He rolled in the direction of the wall. 'Argh!' he cried. 'Help!' Then he went mad in a sticky blizzard that seemed to involve not only sheets, feathers and something like syrup, but quite a lot of furniture as well.

The door opened. A light came on. The voice of his assistant, Otto, said, 'Cor!'

'Summon help!' shrieked Cosm. 'I am under attack!'

'But –'

'Shut up!'

Footsteps thumped. Doors banged. Shins hit furniture. Someone hosed Dr Cosm down. Ten minutes later, he was standing in clean pyjamas and a new dressing gown, allowing the eyes to play over the wreckage of his room. His mind was once again working like a machine of ice and steel. An enemy had done this thing. And he knew which one. When he had become Headmaster and carried out his other plans they would pay. *How* they would pay –

'Better now?' said Otto.

'Shut up!' cried Cosm. 'To the Control Room!'

To the Control Room they went.

'Play this evening's tapes for bedroom AA1A(A),' said Cosm.

Otto pushed buttons. Cosm's bedroom appeared on a screen, white and tranquil.

'Speed it up.'

The whiteness and tranquillity continued for a while. Then, suddenly, the door opened, and a figure in a hooded black robe came in. The face could not be seen.

'Sss,' said Cosm.

The figure held up a box to the CCTV camera.

'Grr,' growled Cosm.

ICEO, said the letters on the box.

'Iceo is icing sugar,' said Otto.

The figure ripped the top off the box, pulled the duvet off the bed, sprinkled a thick layer of icing sugar on the sheet and pulled the duvet neatly back up again.

'Oh I *see*!' cried little Otto. 'So this person puts the soft, soft sugar in your bed and you lie down and you can't feel it but then you go to sleep and you get a teeny bit sweaty so the sugar turns to syrup and you get all sticky and then you wake up and, well, I must say, it is very clever ho ho –'

'Silence!' barked Cosm. 'This wicked miscreant will be punished! Horribly punished, so he will never forget it! I shall inform the Governors and the staff in front of the whole Skool! Perhaps news of this outrage will force the Head to resign!'

'Er . . .' said Otto.

'Your problem, insect?'

'I'm not sure it is a good idea to let it be known . . .'

'*What?*'

'You are a very dignified person,' said Otto, cringing and smarming. 'And of course a possible – that is to say – a future Headmaster. If the Skool were to hear that you had been found screaming for help dressed only in syrup and a layer of goose feathers, they would laugh at you. So would the staff. So would the Governors. Hee.'

'Shut up!'

'Yes, Doctor,' said Otto. 'Hee hee.'

'Ant! Worm!'

'Sorry, master. Hee,' said Otto.

'Sss,' said the Doctor. 'You will see, insect. I have some ideas of my own. Oh, yes, little Svenson, just you *wait!*'

'Yes, Doctor,' said Otto. 'Hee.'

'*What?*'

'Nothing.'

'Good.'

'Hee.'

The Skoolies noticed that the Skolars were extremely cheerful that Thursday morning. In the crowded corridor on the way to breakfast, Rosetti whistled in close harmony with Owen. Onyx, who was a tuneless and spitty whistler, sang along in a high, clear voice:

> '*Oo, Dr Cosm,*
> *Friend of our bosom,*
> *Izzums a problem wozm?*'

Down the corridor they marched. Round the corner they strode. And walked slap into Dr Cosm.

'Ah,' said Cosm, who had sleepless black eyebags above his doughy cheeks. 'Whistling in the corridors. You –' he pointed at Rosetti – 'are obviously the ringleader.' He snapped his fingers. A Security Master came running.

'More Tests?' said Rosetti. 'Lovely. Bring 'em on!'

'No,' said Cosm. 'Take him to the Detention Attic in the Tower.'

'Oo, nasty,' said the Security Master. 'Tower it is, then.'

The Detention Attic was an ancient room with low beams and a window at each side. It smelled terrible, so Rosetti opened the windows. Below him, the Tower sank to the Quad. There were bars on the windows, but very old and rusty ones, and when he pulled one it came away in his hand. But actually the bars were hardly necessary, because it was more than a hundred feet above the ground. No exit that way.

He waited for hours.

At last the door opened.

'Ah, Rosetti,' said the Headmaster's voice. And in he came, accompanied by Dr Cosm and Miss Davies, attempting to look severe and making a bad job of it. 'Hmm,' he said. 'It appears that you have done . . . nothing wrong.'

'Whistling in the corridors,' barked Dr Cosm. 'Bad attitude. Dumb insolence.'

'Is it a problem when I whistle, er, sweetly, sir, hee?' said Rosetti.

'Headmaster, I insist,' said Cosm. 'There is a Governors' Meeting. At which I shall make a full report. Statutes can be changed, you know, in the event of really bad offences.'

'Mmyes,' said the Headmaster. 'Oh, dear, Rosetti. One hates this sort of thing, but Cosm, Governors, difficult . . . it would be better if you stayed here for the next twelve –'

'Twenty-four,' said Cosm.

'– very well, twenty-four hours.'

Rosetti's mouth was hanging open. In a mere eight hours, the doves would be rested enough to zip back through Time to Chartres Cathedral to pick up the Cup. He was needed. Badly. 'But –' he said.

The Headmaster drew himself up to his full height, striking his head on a low beam. 'You have made your bed, and you must lie in it.'

'Not my bed,' said Rosetti, unwisely.

'Leave him!' hissed Cosm. 'The Governors await!'

'I suppose they do,' said Solomon Temple gloomily. 'Ah, well, into the Jaws of Death, what?'

'This is so *unfair*!' said Rosetti, when they had gone.

'You put icing sugar in his bed,' said Miss Davies. 'And then teased him about it. He is a master and you are a pupil so it is your own silly fault. And I can't wait, or the doves will overcharge, and Trym is in a terrible mood nowadays so I can't get new ones out of him, and goodness knows where we'll land up. So you'll have to stay behind.'

She left.

Someone brought bread and water.

Unfair, thought Rosetti, stumping to and fro. Unfair, unfair, *unfair*. He walked to the window and looked out. Pupils milled like ants as the Skool went about its business far below. He might as well not exist. He turned on his heel and went to the window opposite. No busy scene below this one. Just a gargoyle's head that looked like Nurse Drax.

Rosetti went to the food. There were three loaves of bread, marked LUNCH, SUPPER, BREAKFAST. He went to the window and took out a water pistol from his pocket and squirted water at a starling until the starling flew away. He filled the water pistol up with ink from the Detention Inkwell and went back to the window. But no more starlings came near him, and there was no point in squirting stones. He put the water pistol back in his pocket and gazed down the cliff of carved stonework that descended to the scree at the foot of the New-boy's Leap . . .

The cliff of *heavily carved* stonework.

Rosetti tightened his bootlaces. He took a deep breath. He climbed on to the sill of the window that looked away from the Quad. The bars had rusted away. Below him, the Tower narrowed with distance. His mouth was strangely dry. He put a foot out of the window and on to the back of a nearby gargoyle's head. Then he put his other foot on the gargoyle's head. Then he eased his weight off the windowsill and on to his feet, so he was standing on the projection of stone a hundred feet above the ground, and turned round to look at the view.

The gargoyle's head broke off.

Wooo, thought Rosetti, plummeting.

Yank, went something at his back. His shirt was hoiked up under his armpits. He swung, caught by the back of his shirt on another gargoyle, watching two shirt buttons spinning down, down . . .

Pop, went another button. Three to go.

Rosetti raised his hand. The hand found a carving and grasped it. Gradually, he put his weight on it. This one held. He turned and got a foot to another carving. That one held too. Another hand. Another foot. Down he went, down, down. Being Rosetti, he gained confidence as he went. Being Rosetti and in a hurry to catch the dovecote he actually became rather overconfident, and started to scuttle like an ape down the ladder of stone carvings. Lion's head, carved flower, carved branch, bird's wing, lady's shoulder, large block.

On the large block he stood and took a breather.

Until the block fell off.

This time, no handy snag caught his shirt. He fell. But he did not fall for long, because by this time he was only ten feet off the ground.

'Oof!' he said to the patch of grass on which he had landed. It took him a couple of minutes to work out how to breathe. When he had done that he stood up. Bang in ribs, he thought. He fell down. Twisted ankle, he thought. He found a bit of wood to use as a stick and hobbled off towards the dovecote. The ankle got better as he went, but not much. He hid in the box under the chair. His eyes closed. He went to sleep.

Voices woke him. Miss Davies, and Onyx going on about Cathedral Treasuries, and Owen grunting like Owen did. Rosetti kept quiet. He was by no means sure that Miss Davies would approve of death-defying climbs out of detention.

The flap opened. The basket came in. The pole came down. Flap, squawk, nests in the mind.

And the world smelled terrible, and sounded like stone and chanting.

The chair creaked. Rosetti held his breath. The dovecote door opened and closed. Rosetti clambered furtively out of the box and put his eye to a crack in the door. Three figures were standing just outside the door. They were wearing long black cloaks with hoods pulled over their faces. Beyond them, fires burned in a yard, and there was a reek of wood smoke and History. Rosetti rummaged in a basket under the chair, pulled out another robe and put it on.

For a moment he stood quite still.

He could hear something. Not a voice; more a Call, really – faint, but there all the same. The whisper of the Greyte Cup, somewhere nearby –

The whisper stopped like a candle flame blown out.

Outside the dovecote, one of the robed figures began to talk in the clear, bright voice of Miss Davies. 'We find ourselves in the Cathedral Yard,' she said. 'All these people, excuse me, sir, pardon, madam, mind that goat, have come on pilgrimage. Because inside yonder cathedral, yes, Owen, the very big one with the towers and the round arches, is the Skirt of the Virgin Mary and people come from all over the world to see it. It is in the treasure chamber – what is it, Onyx?'

Onyx was saying something.

'Yes, Onyx, you are right. This cathedral does not look like the one in the book. Because it is not the same one. Anyone know why?'

'No,' said Owen. 'The Cup will be in the treasure chamber. Let's go and get it.'

'I know! I know!' said Onyx, bouncing.

Miss Davies sighed. 'Yes?' she said.

'The fire! There was a fire!'

'And the date?'

'1194.'

'What date?'

'Tenth of June,' said Onyx.

Miss Davies squinted narrowly at the position of the sun in relation to the tower that soared into the evening-blue sky. 'Which is actually today,' said Miss Davies.

'They've all come to see the holy relic skirt thing,' said Owen. 'Over here.' He marched off.

'I'll wait near here,' said Miss Davies.

Onyx bounced after Owen and joined him at the end of the line of people shuffling into the great round-arched door of the church. A busker came by, playing a thing like a guitar. Onyx rummaged in her pocket and dropped a small handful of sherbet lemons into his hat and a couple in his mouth. Rosetti sneaked out of the dovecote and stood behind a cart. The busker had fallen to the ground, where he was foaming at the mouth and howling about devils. Rosetti looked at him, but did not really see him. He was tangling with a problem.

Into his mind had come the screams and smoke at the invasion of the Paris Temple – which had been destroyed on the very day the Cup was stolen by Abbot Dagger. And now they had arrived to steal the Cup again, on the very day when it seemed that Chartres Cathedral was destined to burn down. It seemed possible that these frightful events were connected with the stealing of the Cup. Certainly they were disasters. But were they big enough disasters to be classed as Dread Things? And were they happening because the Skolars had arrived? Or were the Skolars arriving because the disasters were happening?

Rosetti's head was hurting again.

He waited until Miss Davies's back was turned. Then he limped away from the cart and into the shadows.

The Holy Skirt queue moved along the great stone nave of the Cathedral, through the fog of incense surrounding the High Altar and down a stone stairway protected by black iron doors. 'The treasure room,' said Owen. They shuffled past a large selection of chalices made of silver and gold. None of them was the Greyte Cup.

People behind them in the queue were pointing at them and whispering. Onyx thought she heard the words 'busker', 'fizzing' and 'demons'. Naturally Owen understood nothing, except that he was getting bored. 'Let's get back to the dovecote,' he said.

But he might as well have been talking to himself. For Onyx was bouncing off down the left-hand side of the church to a wooden scaffolding set against a half-finished window. She scurried up a ladder, and seemed to be talking to one of the workmen.

'Onyx!' hissed Owen.

Onyx slid down to ground level. 'It's all right!' she cried. 'That man's name is François and the window designer is Georges and come *on* his workshop is just out here!'

'Wha,' said Owen.

'That window,' said Onyx, already walking into a maze of lanes. 'It's in the exact same place as the one in the book in the Library, silly! With the picture of the Cup in it! There was a diagram and everything! Only they haven't put the glass in it yet. So Georges the stained-glass window designer has obviously got the Cup in his workshop so he can make an accurate picture of it. He lives first on the left, second on the right, in the Street of the Coughing Sparrow. Here.' She started banging on the door.

Georges was a tall, pale man, not very talkative. He was working on a glass picture of a ship on a sea. Onyx went and stood between him and the frame and tilted her head back. 'Excuse me,' she said in a loud clear voice. 'We are looking for a cup.'

'Go away. I am making window,' said Georges, reaching round her and holding a bit of green glass up next to a bit of light blue glass.

'Not the green,' said Onyx. 'Dark blue would be better.'

Georges' hands flexed in a strangling manner, like the hands of so many people meeting Onyx for the first time.

'We want to see the Cup. *That* Cup,' said Onyx, pointing to a panel of glass in a temporary frame. Owen nodded approvingly. The panel did indeed bear the image of the Greyte Cup.

'You cannot. I have returned the Cup to its owner. Now I said go away,' said Georges.

Onyx folded her arms. 'Not until you tell me where I can find the owner.'

'Agh!' cried Georges. He swore for some time in an unknown dialect, then spat out a sentence in Old French.

'Thank you,' said Onyx. She turned to Owen. 'Well, we've found it. Apparently it belongs to a person called Magnus. At the sign of the Burned Dragon. Over there.' Finger raised, she trotted out of the glass workshop, through the maze of alleys and wove her way between the pilgrims' cooking fires towards the Cathedral wall.

Georges the glassmaker had pointed in the direction of a flight of stone steps that went past a buttress and plunged under the Cathedral. It was a gloomy, threatening place, lit even on this summer evening by flickering orange torches.

'Ooer,' said Onyx, hesitating.

'Come *on*,' said Owen, pushing past her. As far as Owen was concerned, darkness was merely an absence of light.

Twenty yards down the dark passage, a charred-looking carving of a dragon hung over an arch between two fat pillars. The arch was blocked with iron bars.

'Wha?' said a low, gravelly voice from behind them.

'We want to look at your Cup,' said Owen.

'Wha?' said the voice again. Someone behind the bars lifted a torch.

'Eek!' said Onyx.

For the light had fallen on a face that looked like a root vegetable with a disease. It had warts, and hair, and a blob that might have been a nose, and a hole that was definitely a mouth because there was a tooth in it.

'Magnus?' said Owen, who could see no difference between handsome and ugly.

The mouth snarled. Onyx spoke. The mouth spoke back.

'He says that's his name, and who wants to know,

97

and what cup?' said Onyx. 'So I'll draw it! I'll draw it! I've got my crayons!' She whipped out a pad of paper, made a small drawing of the Cup and coloured it in. 'That one!' she said.

The dwarf examined the notebook page. Then he looked up. Suspicion glinted in his only eye. 'How you know it here?' he said.

'We just do,' said Onyx. 'We want to look.'

'Some chance,' said the dwarf scornfully. 'This the Sangrail.' He started to turn away. Then he stopped. 'Whazzat?' he said.

He was looking at Owen, who had taken out his Swiss Army knife and was carving a hard sum on an oak doorpost.

'Swiss Army knife,' said Onyx.

'Want it,' said the dwarf.

Onyx translated. Owen narrowed his eyes. Then he pointed to a chess set on the dwarf's table.

Onyx said, 'You can have Owen's knife if you win. We can have a look at the Cup if Owen wins.'

The dwarf's face split into a frightful grin. He opened the barred door and bowed them into the room. But his eye never left the knife.

Owen slid behind the chess table with the practiced ease of a snake sliding under a bedspread. The dwarf cracked his knuckles, thumped down opposite him and made the first move without asking. Owen countermoved. The board became a blur of move and countermove –

'Hey!' hissed Onyx. 'He cheated!'

'Never mind,' said Owen. Half a dozen big, ugly louts had drifted out of the darkness to watch the game, or anyway to crowd round the table with their eyes fixed hungrily on the Yet-to-be-Invented-Country Army knife. Even Onyx realized that this was probably not a good moment to make a fuss.

There was a final flurry of moves. Owen called, 'Checkmate! Show us the Cup!' and stuffed the knife back in his pocket.

The dwarf sat for a moment with his jaw dropped, his tooth hanging like a yellow Smartie in a cave of darkness.

'He cheated,' said Owen. 'So I cheated back.'

'Gragurrh,' said the dwarf, meaning roughly the same thing. The louts closed in.

Onyx was furious. 'He beat you *fair and square!*' she said in Old French. 'And now you say you want his knife anyway and he can't see the Cup and you are really really horrible and we will all hate you, because this is unfair unfair *unfair*. Plus if you show us the Cup,' she said, remembering to bat her eyelashes a bit, 'I will give you my crayons.'

The dwarf had been squinting in a grim and sarcastic manner. At the mention of crayons, his eyes unsquinted. 'Give,' he said.

'After Cup.'

'Oh.' Pause for messy scratching of head. He

said something. His louts laughed in a not very encouraging way. 'Come.'

The dwarf limped ahead, his shadow vast and lumpy in the torchlight. The procession shambled down vaulted stone passages. The walls closed in. The torches grew less frequent.

The dwarf stopped at last in front of a tiny door made of massive iron and riddled with keyholes. 'Behold!' he cried. He took out a large bunch of keys. 'Turn your backs!' Everyone turned their backs. Iron hinges shrieked. There was a silence. Then the dwarf screamed, a long, terrible scream that echoed in the vault.

'Hm,' said Owen.

The door of the dwarf's strongroom stood open. Torchlight flickered on crowns, sceptres and enamel coffers. But the rough wooden table in the middle was empty, except for a ring in the dust where a cup had stood.

'Gone!' shrieked the dwarf. 'Magnus bin robbed! Aiee!'

Suddenly there was a lot of yelling and grabbing and people asking other people where the Cup had gone, and a smell of mouldy stone, and a clang, and the sound of bolts shooting, muffled by the thickness of a door. Then there was darkness, and silence except for the sound of breathing. 'Are we here?' said Owen.

'I am,' said a patch of darkness, using the voice

of Onyx. 'I think there's just us and we're in a d-dungeon.'

'Quite a deep one, by the smell of it,' said Owen.

'Perhaps we'll get rescued,' said Onyx.

'We are a hundred and ten feet below ground level, eight hundred and fourteen years away from Skool,' said Owen. 'Nobody knows where we are. Not even Miss Davies because she is hanging around the dovecote.'

'Oh.'

Silence.

'Plus the Cathedral is due to burn down any minute now.'

'Oo,' said Onyx, in a small, high voice.

'Perhaps we'll get out. But it's not very likely.'

'Ee,' said Onyx, even smaller and higher.

'Impossible actually,' said Owen, after a short pause to think it over.

'Ik,' said Onyx, in an absolutely minute bat-like squeak.

Silence fell.

6

Rosetti had not bothered to join the relic queue, but had followed his fellow Skolars at a distance, moving carefully because of his bad ankle. He had hung around in the shadows outside the glassmaker's shop. He had not liked the look of the underground passage, but he had felt he ought to follow. Then sure enough there were Owen and Onyx being hustled down a dark tunnel by five louts and a dwarf, and a scream, and an iron door slamming. Rosetti pressed himself into an alcove as the louts and the dwarf came back without the Skolars. The louts stationed themselves at the end of the passage while the dwarf stumped off to book a torture chamber.

Squashed into his little patch of shadow, Rosetti thought hard. To help his classmates he would have to get past the louts. The louts had weapons. Primitive weapons, true, but extremely sharp.

What to do?

Rosetti allowed himself to imagine that the louts

were Security Masters, and the Cathedral Crypt was Skool. What would he have done?

Easy.

Reaching under his robe, he pulled out the water pistol. He marched up to the largest of the louts. 'Oi!' he cried. 'Mutton face!' The lout looked up, ready to maim. A jet of something hit his eye. The eye started stinging. He licked at what was running down his face. It tasted vile. He wiped his face with his hand and saw by the torchlight that the stuff was blue.

Even in a world where water pistols are easy to get hold of, people are surprised when squirted in the eye with ink. In a world where water pistols had not yet been invented, Rosetti had suspected that the effect would be pretty intense.

He was not disappointed.

'Aiee!' cried the lout. 'Witchcraft!' A knife hurtled through the air and clattered off the wall in the exact spot where Rosetti had been standing. But Rosetti was no longer there. He was limping down a side-tunnel, taking the wall-torches down from their brackets and throwing them behind him as he ran. His ankle hurt. But Rosetti limping was faster than most people running. He could hear the louts lumbering after him.

He passed two doorways on his right, and tossed a torch into the second. When he came to a third, he turned down it and waited. The lumbering came closer. He held his breath. If they looked in on him, he was doomed.

But the lumbering went off down the side-alley where he had thrown the torch. He let out his breath. He heard voices, large and stupid, fading into a hollow distance. He threaded through the passages back towards the Skolars' dungeon. A lot of red light was pouring out of an archway, together with heat and smoke. The guards must have been doing some torch-throwing of their own. By the light of the flames he caught a glimpse of a wooden scaffolding of the kind that might support a cathedral floor.

He arrived in the central passage. It was getting quite smoky. Snatching up a torch, he started for the narrow entrance to the dungeon tunnel. Then, seized by an afterthought, he yelled, '*Fire! Fuego! Feuer! Fuoco! Conflagratio! Incendie! Au feu!*' and heard the cry taken up all through the warren of wood and stone.

Onyx and Owen were sitting in silence when they smelled smoke and heard muffled shouting. 'It's started,' squeaked Onyx. 'What shall we *do*?'

Owen felt he should say something, but he did not know what. He cleared his throat anyway, in case he had an idea at the last minute.

The bolts creaked.

The door swung open.

'Oo!' cried Onyx.

'Who?' cried Owen.

'It's only me,' said the voice of Rosetti. 'I think we'd better go. I mean the place seems to be on fire and the guards will be back any minute, so on the whole . . .'

'Run!' squeaked Onyx.

'Walk,' said Rosetti, whose ankle was now hurting quite badly. 'Sing.'

The louts came back out of the tunnel coughing, spluttering and very annoyed. As they stumped into the main passage, three small Grey Friars walked past them, hoods pulled down, chanting in the language the Grey Friars used.

'Stop 'em,' said the Chief Lout. 'Take a look under those hoods.'

'Oh, yeah,' said the Second Lout. 'Like it'll do any good. And like your britches aren't on fire.'

'Me? Fire? Britches? Aiee!' cried the Chief Lout, realizing the truth of this remark. And the louts lost interest in the Friars, because they were busy putting the Chief's trousers out by dipping him in a nearby privy.

'All my eye and Betty Martin, All my eye and Betty Martin,' sang the Skolars, climbing the steps from the crypt and marching across the churchyard between the pilgrim fires. 'All my eye and –'

'In,' said Miss Davies, gliding out of the shadows

and unlocking the dovecote door. 'Goodness! Rosetti! What are you doing here?'

'Being useful,' said Owen. 'No Cup, though. Already stolen.'

'Stolen?'

'We'd better hurry,' said Onyx.

Dusk had fallen. The churchyard was lit with a hard orange light, and the round-arched windows were pouring flame.

The dovecote door closed. A flap of wings. Nests in the mind. 'We're back,' said Miss Davies.

Nobody moved. They lay flopped in the chair, minds full of fire and heat and the remains of fear.

Rosetti said, 'I started that fire. Or I did the thing that made the lout throw the torch that started it, so without me there wouldn't have been one. Except –' he was looking at Miss Davies – 'all these horrible things keep happening. The invasion of the Temple. The burning of the Cathedral.'

'So what we wonder,' said Owen, amazingly, 'is whether all this Cup stealing is stretching Time.'

'And causing sort of explosions in History,' said Onyx. 'Sort of Dread Things.'

'Goodness,' said Miss Davies, looking solemn. 'You *have* been sleeping in the knife drawer. But what's the most important thing?'

'To find the Cup so the Dread Thing doesn't happen, then win it so the Head doesn't get sacked and Dr Cosm doesn't take over.'

'Exactly.' Miss Davies glanced at her watch. 'Zounds, is that the time? Rosetti, you must rush back to the Detention Attic!'

'Right,' said Rosetti. It seemed that if you spent an hour in History an hour passed in Present Time. Otherwise you would get younger. Or something. His head was beginning to hurt again. Quickly, he tumbled out of the dovecote and hobbled away towards the Tower of Flight.

Miss Davies and Onyx and Owen walked across the kitchen garden towards the Cloisters. Onyx and Owen were rather quiet. They had travelled eight hundred and fourteen years, been cheated at chess, threatened with sharp weapons, locked in a dungeon and rescued by sheer luck. They had also watched one of the greatest cathedrals in the world catch fire, and failed in a vital errand.

'Ah!' cried a voice. 'Oh! I say!' And there was the Headmaster, wading towards them through the asparagus bed, beaming, his black gown flapping like a crow's wings. 'How did it go?' said the Head.

'We all got back in one piece,' said Miss Davies.

'Thank goodness,' said the Head. 'And . . . the other?'

'The Cup?' Miss Davies shook her head. 'I'm sorry. Someone got there first.'

'Ah, well,' said the Head, looking (Onyx thought) deeply downcast. 'Better luck next time, what?' He pulled a vast watch from his pocket. 'Oh dear,' he said. 'You've missed supper. Tell you what, though. I've got some haunch of venison and apple pie that needs eating. How about it?'

'Yes, please,' said Onyx and Owen both together.

They ate a delicious supper in the Head's richly decorated apartment while he told them extremely interesting facts about human sacrifice in Ancient Assyria.

Afterwards, Owen said, 'Would you mind if I went and practised some Hard Sums?'

'Be my guest,' said the Head.

'And I'll get to the Library,' said Onyx.

'Still on the Cup hunt?'

'Of course.'

The Head's kindly brow clouded. 'Tell you what,' he said. 'Come with me.' He strode off, his legs scissoring him along at such a clip that Onyx had to run to keep up. He led her up a spiral staircase to a small but comfortable room containing an armchair and a telescope. 'Sordid, to spy on one's colleagues,' said the Head. 'But necessary, alas. Take a look.'

Onyx peered into the telescope's eyepiece. She was looking into a small room. There was a table and two chairs. On one of the chairs sat Dr Cosm. On the other sat the Librarian. Dr Cosm was saying something to the Librarian, who was giggling a servile giggle. The two men raised their hands and high-fived. A grin of evil triumph split Cosm's suety features.

'Oo!' cried Onyx, shocked.

'So I very much fear,' said the Head, 'that when you take a book out of the Library, the Librarian will tell Cosm what it was. If you want something to be private, don't let the Librarian get wind of it. That man Cosm has promised him that on the day he becomes Head the Librarian will get a huge pay rise and hundreds of computers and that he will be allowed to burn all the books.'

'Burn *books*?' said Onyx, even more shocked.

'He hates them. Asthma.'

'Oh.'

'Well, I am counting on you,' said the Head. 'I know you'll find out what's going on. And, even more important, that you'll find the Cup.'

'We will!' cried Onyx, burning with sympathy for this very nice Headmaster surrounded by creeps. 'Never fear, Headmaster, we will!'

Next morning it was cold on the parade ground, and it had rained in the night, so the Duggan Cube stood reflected in a great black puddle. In the puddle stood the whole Skool, dressed in navy-blue shorts and thin shirts and shivering as the rainwater soaked through their canvas gym shoes. The whole Skool was about to do PE practice for Founder's Day –

Not quite the whole Skool.

In the Duggan Cube control room, Dr Cosm sat in front of an electric fire, watching his screen. Onyx was reading a book, and had forgotten about such silly little matters as Whole Skool PE. The camera was trying to peer over her shoulder. But the writing was blurred by dust in the air.

'Curses,' piped Otto.

'It is not important,' said Cosm in a voice both chilly and grim. 'We will find out where they were going by some other method. And we will take action.'

'Nyahahahaha,' said Otto.

'Shut up,' said Cosm.

Actually it would not have done Cosm any good if he had been able to see over Onyx's shoulder. She was taking it easy, waiting for the pigeons to recharge. The book she was reading was called *Astonishing Facts About Coleoptera*. A shadow fell across the page.

'Gosh,' said Onyx, without looking up. 'Did you know that the Bombardier Beetle can squirt boiling oil out of its bottom? Crazee, eh?'

'We are not amazed,' said a voice that reeked of gin.

'Ooer,' said Onyx, slamming the book, sitting up and turning round. And there towering above her was Mato.

'Young ladies do not read about er rude beetles,'

said Mato. 'Young ladies do Whole Skool PE with Founder's Day Marching Practice.'

'Oh gosh,' said Onyx.

'Nonsense,' said a sparkling voice. 'Beetles? Marvellous. Just as I instructed you, Onyx.' And there was Miss Davies, beaming upon Matron with the full golden power of her eyes.

'But marching,' said Mato. 'All pupils must –'

'Fiddle!' cried Miss Davies.

'I shall report this rude slackness to Dr Cosm,' hissed Mato like a ginny serpent.

'And I am sure the Head will be thrilled to hear about such devotion to Study,' said Miss Davies brightly. 'Come, Onyx. It is time for you to perform your busy tasks.'

'Yes, Miss Davies.' Oo, thought Onyx. Squish, Mato! Juice!

When they were out of sight of Mato, Miss Davies said, 'OK, concentrate. I need another recorded sighting of the Cup. Pronto!'

'Coming up!' cried Onyx, bouncing back to the Library.

High in the Duggan Cube in front of the screens, Dr Cosm said to the Librarian, 'There she goes! Get after her!'

'Must I?'

'Will you let a little puff of dust stand in my way?'

'Yes, Doctor,' said the Librarian, wheezing already. 'That is to say, no, Doctor.'

'Run!' said Otto.

'Shut up!' said Cosm.

Up in the Library, the wheelbarrow rumbled around the aisles at breakneck speed. The cloud of dust billowed from Onyx's corner. And from the middle of the cloud came a shrill, bouncy cry of 'Ha!'

'Ha wha?' wheezed the Librarian.

Something rushed out of the dust cloud. It seemed to be Onyx, moving fast.

'Books are not to be removed from the –'

The door slammed. Feet thundered downstairs.

'– Library,' said the Librarian, commencing a coughing fit.

'Look!' cried Onyx, slamming the books on the Skolary table. 'Hot Cup stuff! I brought all the emperor books to muddle Libo but it says here that Emperor Valentinian the Third was a sporting sort of emperor keen on Harpastum which was a kind of football and archery and a great collector of treasure – listen to this – *particularly cups.*'

'So?' said Rosetti. He was in a bad mood after marching, particularly because Slee and Damage Duggan had spent the whole practice trying to stamp on his bad ankle.

'What is engraved on the Greyte Cup's knop?'

'Valentinianus III, of course. Get on with it,' said Owen. He had not enjoyed the marching either.

'Why would Valentinian's name be on the Cup?'

'Because it belonged to him?'

'Exactly! And Rome was invaded by the Vandals in the last year of his reign. Ideal Cup-stealing conditions. So all we've got to do is go back to Rome in, what, AD 455 and take the Cup and bring it back.'

'Easy as that,' said Rosetti, highly sarcastic.

'I expect it will be most educational,' said Miss Davies. 'But slightly dangerous. I mean it does mean getting mixed up with the early stages of the Looting of Rome.'

'Dangerous?' said Rosetti. 'Compared to Marching and Slee and Damage Duggan?'

'See what you mean,' said Miss Davies. 'Well, the Time Doves could be ready the day after tomorrow. I asked Trym for some extras, but he seems to be very angry about something and there's no talking to him. Fed up with my father stepping in chamber pots, probably. He always was fussy.'

'Not so fast,' said Rosetti. 'I've been thinking. There's something wrong. You said all that about Time being like a river and eating a slice of bread being a small eddy that disappears but stealing a crown being a big thing that tries to divide Time and tears reality and makes a Dread Thing happen. Well, the Greyte Cup is just as important as a crown. And it keeps on getting nicked but no Dread Thing happens. I mean someone stole it from Magnus but it still landed up with the Templars. So it was sort of in two Time streams at once. But no Dread Thing happened.' His head was beginning to hurt again, but he ploughed on. 'So either what you're saying about Time streams is not true. Or the Greyte Cup isn't real.'

'But I've seen it!' said Onyx. 'And so's Owen. And Owen can't see anything that isn't real. Do you dream, Owen?'

'Whaddayamean, dream?'

'See?'

'Right,' said Rosetti, who could feel Miss Davies's eyes burning into him. 'So what I think is this. The Cup talks to me. So there is something special about it. And what I think is that it is real and not real at the same time. The Novice Master in the Temple said it was the Holy Grail. The dwarf Magnus called it the Sangrail, which is another name for the same thing.'

'Holy Grail wha?' said Owen.

'The Holy Grail is a great and sacred cup. A legendary cup. The object of the greatest quests in history and legend,' said Onyx in a strange, awestruck voice.

'So the Greyte Cup for Achievement really definitely is the Holy Grail,' said Rosetti.

Miss Davies shrugged. 'I should have known there was no point in trying to hide anything from Polymathic Skolars,' she said. 'Yep, that's it.'

There was a long, stunned silence. It was Miss Davies who broke it. 'Now listen closely,' she said, 'because this is not easy. There is only one stream of Time, remember. A thing can't be in two places at once, if it is a thing like this crown that we all keep talking about. But Rosetti is right, the Grail is different. On the one hand, it's a real gold cup. On the other, it's a myth, and a legend, which is another way of saying it's a story. A cup can't be in more than one place at a time. But a story can. A story can have millions of different versions all existing at the same time. So I think that the part of the Greyte Cup that's a story makes it easier for the Cup to travel around in Time without causing Dread Things to happen. But the part of the Greyte Cup that's real means that every time it's moved around in time, a small sort of Dread Thing happens, like the Temple being overwhelmed, or the Cathedral burning.

'The Dread Things are small because the Cup has very little effect on History when it is locked away in treasure chambers and secret rooms, and of course most people who had anything to do with the Cup don't survive the mini-Dread Things, so its history starts again. But if isn't in the Sealed Room when the Head goes to get it on Founder's Day . . . well. The Head gets the sack and Cosm takes over the Skool. That's an effect. And you know what we saw in the Examinator. That's what happens.'

'And there's something else, isn't there?' said Rosetti.

'Oh?'

'I read somewhere that the holder of the Grail is meant to get absolute power.'

Miss Davies looked shocked.

'Tell us everything,' said Rosetti.

'Go on!' cried Onyx eagerly.

'Is there a problem?' said Owen.

'Oh, all right. Rosetti's right. There are legends, that's all. That the Holder of the Grail becomes Master of the Universe. Master of Time and Space and all that sort of stuff. Probably nonsense.'

'Or possibly not,' said Rosetti.

'Quite. So we'd better find it before . . .'

'It falls into the wrong hands,' said Rosetti.

'Cosm's hands,' said Onyx.

'Cosm as Master of the Universe?' said Owen. 'Yuk.'

'And he would misuse his power.'

Into the minds of all came the view in the Examinator; the stagnant lake with the scaly green necks twining against a background of jungly mountains.

'Ooer,' said Onyx.

116

'Now then,' said Miss Davies. 'Two days till dove readiness. It's time we all did some work, because there's a Greyte Cup to win, and only just over two weeks to win it in! Books together. Pencils sharp. Lessons. Off you go!'

And off went the Skolars, into the thunder of boots on floors as Abbot Dagger's Academy went to classes.

Two days later. Sixteen centuries earlier. Creak of wicker, coo of doves, flap, squawk, nests in the mind.

Miss Davies said, 'Robes on, and be careful.'

'I've been to Rome before,' said Rosetti. 'I mean after. With my parents. They were stealing some statues.'

'How very wrong,' said Miss Davies. 'Be careful, now. I'll wait here.'

Outside the door the sun was blinding, the air hot and smelly. The dovecote had as usual landed in an out-of-the-way corner. From beyond a small thicket of dried-up scrub smoke was rising.

Rosetti pointed at a collection of tall white buildings on a cliff. 'That's the Capitoline Hill.' He set off through the undergrowth. The Skolars followed.

Their hooded robes looked somewhat different from the tunics of the locals, but nobody stared. Actually the locals seemed to have other things on their minds. They were standing around in groups, casting nervous glances to the west, where the blue of the sky was muddied by smoke. Rosetti led the Skolars through a half-ruined tangle of lanes to the back of an enormous building of grubby white marble. They crept round the wall until they found a gate. There were sentry boxes. The boxes were empty. There was a sort of huddle of men in armour in the square in front of the building, with a man in the middle pointing to the west and waving his arms.

'Imperial Palace,' said Rosetti. Through the gate they went, across the palace yard, up steps and under a portico, following the brightest tiles and the richest gilding, stepping out of the way of hurrying, worried-looking people.

After ten minutes' hard walking they had passed through the palace, and were standing on the edge of a great open area of ground with a goal at either end and twenty-odd men scattered around in the middle.

'A football pitch!' said Owen.

One of the footballers was taller than the others, with yellow hair and a face like a goldfish. 'Mine!' he cried, barging a member of his own side out of the way, taking a mighty hack at a ball, missing and falling on his bottom.

'Oh well *played*!' cried the other players, rather wearily.

Rosetti stiffened. 'It's here,' he said.

'What is?'

'The Cup.'

'Where?'

'Can't tell. But close.'

Goldfish face got up, scowled with concentration, kicked, missed, but made contact on the backswing. The ball trickled backwards into a goal.

'Goal!' said Onyx, bouncing and clapping.

'*Own* goal,' said Rosetti.

'No,' said Onyx. 'They are saying that it was half time just after he kicked it so they changed ends so it is a goal for his team.'

'The score is now 213–0,' cried a scorer.

'213–1,' said Goldfish face with a great show of fairness.

'Oo yes,' said the other players, bowing. 'Your Imperial Majesty is indeed noble and sporting. 213–*1*.'

Rosetti said, 'I wonder if that geezer with the yellow hair is by any chance the Emperor.'

'How did you *guess*?' said Onyx.

'Mind your backs!' cried a man clanking past with a wheelbarrow full of gold and jewels.

'Treasure!' said Owen.

'In a *barrow*?'

'Look,' said Rosetti, pointing.

Beyond the football pitch the ground sloped westward to the crowded houses of Rome. Among the houses curled a wide, yellowish river. On the river there floated ships: black ships, their sides lined with shields, with low square sails the colour of dried blood.

'They don't look very Roman,' said Owen.

'Oh for goodness' *sake*,' said Onyx, with a really annoying sniff. 'This is March 455, just before the Looting of Rome, when the bad wicked nasty barbarian Vandals were beginning to sail their ships up the Tiber and loot the Eternal City.'

'The wha?'

'Rome. So those people are Vandals and that haze in the sky is smoke and the wheelbarrows are moving the Emperor's treasure so the Vandals do not nick it and actually the Vandals will be here any minute now.'

'While the Emperor plays football,' said Rosetti.

'He was very keen on football,' said Onyx. 'And not very bright. And very very doomed.'

'So let's go and get the Cup before some Vandal comes and swipes it,' said Owen. 'It's probably down here.' He trotted off after the barrow. The others followed him.

They arrived in a sort of loading bay under the palace. Men were packing treasure into a cart. A small man in a cream-coloured robe was standing alongside, ticking off items on a wax tablet.

'Keep out of the way, shorty,' said a large,

dim-looking man with Security Guard written all over him. 'Nothing 'ere for you.'

'But I am the Keeper and Guardian of the Treasure!' cried the man.

'Tell that to the Vandals,' said the Security Man. 'If they'll listen, hur, hur.'

'Onyx!' said Rosetti. 'Tell this Keeper that it is a great honour to meet him, and that news of his learning has spread as far as Britannia.'

'But it hasn't.'

'It has now. And tell him we would like to admire the Cup.'

Onyx was already talking. The Keeper listened, frowning. Then his eyes lit up and he started to jabber and his hands traced in the air the outline of a goblet that was unmistakably the Greyte Cup, otherwise the Holy Grail.

'He says he is delighted you have such good taste,' said Onyx, translating. 'For this is an ancient cup that survived the doom of drowned Atlantis. Of course it has been a bit spoiled when the silly Emperor had his name engraved upon the knop. But he would be delighted to show it to us. It is just over there.'

The Keeper shouted an order at the packers. And suddenly there was a packer standing up, and there in his hand, glittering in the hot Roman sun, was the Greyte Cup.

'Grab it!' said Owen.

'Be subtle,' said Rosetti, pushing his spiky-haired colleague gently but firmly behind him. 'And get ready to run.' Then, to the Keeper, 'Atlantean, you say? I should have said earlier.'

'No, no,' said the Keeper. 'Certainly it has the metals and shape of Atlantis.'

'Show me,' said Rosetti, putting out his hands. The Keeper handed him the Cup.

'ARRRRRRRRR,' cried a great voice somewhere. There was a tramp of nailed shoes. A squad of large barbarians came round the corner at a run. There was a roar of noise and a blur of movement and a cluster of sweaty faces grinning with effort and painted blue, perhaps with woad. The lead barbarian was wearing a tunic bearing the device of a dagger. It looked like a Footer shirt. A Skool Footer shirt. The squad rushed between Rosetti and the Keeper and ran on. A smaller man was bringing up the rear. He looked round. Onyx could not see his face properly, but she could have sworn that he had an extra eye in the middle of his forehead.

The Keeper stood with his mouth open and his hands outstretched, as if he had just handed Rosetti the Cup. Rosetti stood with his mouth open and his hands outstretched, as if he was about to receive the Cup. But neither of them had the Cup.

The Cup was gone.

'After them!' yelled Onyx.

'Guards!' yelled the Keeper.

'Careful!' yelled Rosetti.

'That was a Dagger Footer shirt! Those were Games Skoolies!' yelled Owen.

'Those aren't!' yelled Onyx, pointing.

A group of men in horned helmets were running towards them. Some were waving swords, others axes.

'Vandals. Ooer,' said Onyx, summing up the general view.

'Gentlemen, gentlemen!' cried the Keeper, stepping in front of the Vandals and standing there on wobbly knees. 'Just in time! Here you will see the er treasure of the Emperor, all packed up and ready to go! Provided you put it on public display obviously!'

'Display?' said the lead Vandal. 'Course we will, we'll show it to our wives. Outta the way, fungus face.'

'Rrrr!' cried the Vandals, and dived into the cart with an expensive clanking noise.

'Off we go,' said Rosetti in a very small voice.

'What about the Cup?' said Owen.

'Cups are no good to people who have been chopped up with axes,' said Rosetti.

'See what you mean. Keeper, I should run if I were you.'

The Skolars tiptoed away. 'What will the Emperor *say?*' moaned the Keeper, already running.

'Goal!' said the large, silly voice of the Emperor from beyond a pall of smoke.

'Hmm,' said the Keeper, disappearing over the horizon.

The Skolars slunk back to the patch of scrub, dodging a couple of Vandal patrols carrying bulging sacks. And there was the dovecote.

'No Cup?' said Miss Davies, looking up from the Time Dove she was feeding.

'I had it in my hand,' said Rosetti.

'It was snatched,' said Onyx.

'By Footerers,' said Owen. 'From our own time.'

'I saw Slee,' said Onyx.

'And Damage,' said Rosetti.

'Impossible. In. Quick,' said Miss Davies.

A gust of smoke eddied through the dovecote. Cries in Vandalese came from outside. 'Off we go,' said Miss Davies as something thunked into the door.

Flutter, coo, nest thoughts. The smoke had gone. From outside came the distant cries of Games sufferers and the familiar pong of Skool.

'To the Study,' said Miss Davies. They waded through the other Skoolies. When they were sitting down, she said, 'Tell me what happened.'

'We had the Cup nearly in our hands,' said Rosetti. 'But it was snatched away. By Slee. And Damage. I told you.'

'You are imagining things,' said Miss Davies. 'How would those idiots travel in Time?'

'Dunno,' said Owen doggedly. 'But they did.'

Miss Davies smiled. 'I think not,' she said. 'The art of Time voyaging has vanished since my father's time. You must have been seeing things.'

'Not necessarily,' said Owen, and opened his mouth to start arguing.

Onyx knew that if he started he would never stop, so she cut him off. 'The Keeper said it came from Atlantis. It must have survived the Drowning, come through Jerusalem and arrived in Rome.'

'Atlantis, eh?' said Miss Davies. 'I always thought it was mythical. Well, time for prep.'

'Slee and –'

'You'll be late!' trilled Miss Davies, and waltzed from the room.

The Skolars washed off the grime of burning Rome. Then they climbed into Skool Uniform and marched up to Big Skool and took their places. Elphine was there. She had blue dye on her face.

'You're all inky,' said Onyx.

'Never,' said Elphine.

'You're blue,' said Onyx, pointing.

'That was off of Slee's hand,' said Elphine dreamily. 'He walloped me one. Slee's fantastic,' she said.

'Oh,' said Onyx, peering at the blue dye. It was not ink. It was woad. As worn by Vandals at the Sack of Rome.

'You got a boyfriend yet?' said Elphine.

'Two,' said Onyx, blushing violently. Her heart was hammering too. But that was nothing to do with fibs about boyfriends. It was because this was proof that Slee had been in Rome.

After Prep was Tea. People threw food while Security Masters patrolled the aisles writing names in notebooks. Founder's Day was a mere twelve days away, and everyone was pretty excited, except for Onyx and Rosetti and Owen, who were rather worried, and threw food to stop themselves thinking about it.

'They were in Rome,' said Onyx, ducking to avoid the blizzard of flung buns. 'I've got evidence.'

'Wha?' Rosetti tossed a pat of butter at the ceiling, where it clung.

'Slee and Damage.'

'So you keep saying,' said Rosetti. 'But like Miss Davies said: how would they get there?'

'They must have a machine.'

'Never,' said Rosetti. 'Two, in the same Skool?'

'I tell you, they're finding out where we are going in Time and getting there before us and nicking the Cup.'

'They can't be,' said Rosetti. 'Because if they had nicked the Cup before us, it wouldn't have been there for us to see. Ow.'

'Wha.'

'My head hurts.'

'Well, someone's nicking it,' said Owen, logical as always. 'And we did see it, and no Dread Thing has happened. The reason for this is as follows. One, it is always nicked just before it would have disappeared anyway, in the storming of the Temple or the Chartres fire or the Sack of Rome. And like Miss Davies said, it's half real and half legend, so the normal rules do not apply.'

'This is not logical.'

'But it is true, because I have seen it,' said Owen, 'so it must be logical, but in a way we do not yet understand. The other logical thing is that someone else has got a Time Machine, and they know where we're going, and they get there first. And I did see Slee and Damage and they are Dr Cosm's favourites, so I think it is Dr Cosm. And I'm going to look for their machine. Tonight.'

The butter pat on the ceiling had been melting steadily. Now it dropped on the head of a Security Master.

'Nice shot,' said Owen, and trudged away.

As Rosetti watched him go, this thought was in his head:

Onyx had a mind like a firework display, brilliant, but shooting in all directions. Owen was different. He had never, ever known Owen to be wrong.

7

At ten o'clock, half an hour after lights out, Owen
sat up. In the next bed Rosetti was breathing evenly.
Owen put on his dressing gown, pulled a paper
bag with eyeholes over his head, and padded silently
out of the room. Hong, phew, snored Rosetti as
Owen closed the door.

Owen went along the corridor and trotted down
the stairs. He ducked into an alcove to let a master
crunch by. Then he flitted out into the Cloisters.

A three-quarter moon was hanging in a slate-
black sky. Shadows lay jagged across the grey grass,
and the Duggan Cube was the colour of bone.
Owen flitted from shadow to shadow until he was
in the Cube porch.

He gimmicked the keypad (easy, to one of his
giant mind) and pushed open the door. Inside, the
corridors were lit pale blue. He paused, listening.
Was that a footfall behind him? Silence, except for
the distant hum of pumps and the roar of his
breath inside the paper bag.

On the video screens in the Control Room, the small figure padded down the corridor and made a rude sign at the camera. But Otto was asleep at the console, dreaming of his new life as Deputy Headmaster of the Universe. And Dr Cosm was in his white bed, snoring behind his new locks, dreaming of Tests.

Or so Owen hoped.

Owen had no idea what a Time Machine looked like. But there was nothing that could possibly have been one in any of the classrooms. Silently, he checked the Control Room. It smelled of sleeping Otto. He checked the labs. Nothing. He went down to the cellars. They stretched away far and empty under the dim lights, as tidy as only Dr Cosm could make them. Nothing there either. There was only one place left.

He took a narrow steel staircase that wound into the very core of the Cube. A door ahead of him said HIGH ENERGY PHYSICS LAB – KEEP OUT.

'No,' said Owen. He gripped the door handle and pushed it down. There was a *clunk* of precision machinery. The door swung open. He went in, leaving the door open.

The High Energy Physics Laboratory was bigger on the inside than on the outside. On the steel floor under the blue lights stood a table surrounded by six chairs. All were made out of a pale-grey metal that did not reflect the lights. In the middle of the table was something that looked like a flower vase with no flowers in it. Owen stooped over the table to examine the vase. A sound made him look up.

The door was closing.

He leaped across the room and tried to push it open. But it was too powerful for him, and it clunked shut.

Owen sat down on one of the metal chairs. Telling lies made him feel really, really ill. What would he do when Dr Cosm came in tomorrow morning and asked him what he was doing? It would be awful. And there was another thing. Owen had read a book once. In the book someone had got stuck in a place and it had been silly because the shut-up person had been there for days but he had never needed the lavatory. Owen needed the lavatory now. He looked around. He spotted the vase thing in the middle of the table. He emptied it out and put it on the floor –

The door was opening.

'Psst,' said a voice.

Owen looked up, heart hammering. He saw Rosetti, dressed like him in dressing gown, pyjamas and paper bag.

'Quick!' cried Owen, and sprinted out of the door and into the lavatory.

Rosetti took a look around the High Energy Lab. The door was closing again, slowly. He put the vase back on the table and slid out into the corridor. Owen came out of the lav. Rosetti said, 'I hope you didn't flush the –'

The corridor filled with a huge roar of flushing.

'– bog,' said Rosetti. 'Run!'

A door slammed upstairs. Otto had woken up. Now he was pressing buttons. Sirens began to sound.

They ran out of the labs, dived through the outer door as it closed, sprinted across the Cloisters and up to their dorm. They flung their paper bags into the waste-paper basket, leaped into their beds and closed their eyes.

Two minutes later the dorm door opened. They heard heavy footsteps and smelled the reeking breath of Dr Cosm. Then to Rosetti's intense relief Miss Davies's voice rang like silver bells upon the air. 'Doctor?' she said. 'Hello. A charming evening, is it not?'

'There has been trespassing,' said Dr Cosm. 'Alarms have sounded. Paper bags have been worn on heads to evade CCTV.'

'Nothing to do with my Skolars,' said Miss Davies primly. 'My Skolars know how to behave. Perhaps it was your nasty science people –'

'Not nasty,' said Dr Cosm. 'Rigorous. Correct.'

'Whatever,' said Miss Davies. 'Now I think you should trot along. Goodnight.'

'Sss,' said Dr Cosm, like a defeated serpent, and left.

Miss Davies came into the dorm. She went to the waste-paper basket, pulled out the paper bags and tore them into tiny fragments, then sat on the chair between Owen's and Rosetti's beds. She said, 'Well?'

'I told you. I saw the Duggans in Rome,' said Owen. 'And Onyx saw Slee's woad on Elphine. I went to look for their Time Machine.'

'And I followed him,' said Rosetti. 'Just in case. Because he can't tell lies and I can.'

'Teamwork. Excellent,' said Miss Davies absently. 'Time Machine, though? How *could* they?'

'Dunno, but they must have,' said Owen, stubbornly. 'They were there. Look at this.' Owen put something into Miss Davies's hand. Rosetti passed her his reading-under-the-bedclothes torch.

'Yes?' said Miss Davies from above the pool of yellow torchlight.

'It is a coin,' said Owen. 'I found it when I emptied the vase on the table. It is a five-sesterce piece bearing on one side the head of Valentinian the Third. The one we saw playing football one thousand five hundred and fifty-three years ago this morning. Look,' said Owen. 'It is brand new.'

There was a silence. Then Miss Davies said, 'Golly.'

Then there was a really long silence, because Rosetti and Owen had gone to sleep.

As the Skool clock boomed nine the next morning, the Librarian raised gloomy eyes from his catalogue. The little enemy girl was here again, all clean and shiny in the morning sun, her pigtails sticking out like the hands of a clock at twenty past four. The Librarian knew her name was Onyx Keene, but that was not what the Librarian called her. What the Librarian called her was Asthma Attack.

'Morning, Libo!' cried Onyx, dumping her notebook in her usual corner and pulling a wheelbarrow out of the rack. 'Where's all the Ancient Egypt?'

The Librarian pointed dumbly, his handkerchief pressed to his face. 'If you want me,' he said indistinctly, 'I shall be on the windowsill in the nice fresh air.'

The barrow rumbled. From his perch on the windowsill, the Librarian watched Onyx plunge sneezing into the dust drifts. Pages began to turn and dust to billow. From the cloud came cries of 'Atishoo!' and 'Ptshah!' And, finally, 'Yeahchoo!' followed by the thump of feet heading down the Tower's stairs.

Interesting, thought the Librarian, who knew his shelves well. Asthma Attack had said Ancient Egypt. But she had actually taken the books on

Atlantis. Obviously she was trying to mislead him. Ahahaha, thought the Librarian, reaching for the telephone and dialling Dr Cosm.

'Very interesting,' said Dr Cosm. 'When I achieve Absolute Power you will profit from this, Librarian. Benefits and rebates will accrue. Oh yes indeed. Nyahahaha.'

'Nyahahahaha,' said the Librarian.

'Shut up,' said Dr Cosm.

Next morning it was time to hand in the Lovely Writing part of the Greyte Cup work. This was Onyx's responsibility. Of course she had finished her poem, an Ode to Wisdom, three days ago. Since there were a couple of hours before handing-in time, she concentrated on colouring in the capital letters. Thus it was not until the lesson after Break that the Skolars were able to have discussions in the Study.

Miss Davies started. She said, 'About other Time Machines. I've checked the pigeons. There are none missing. And nobody else has the skills.'

'What is the motto of the Polymathic Skolar?' said Rosetti cheekily.

Onyx's hand shot up. 'There is more than one explanation for everything!' she cried.

'Including Time Travel,' said Rosetti.

'Also there are more ways of getting ancient coins than fetching them from the past,' said Miss Davies.

'Now. Do your research, Onyx. Because as soon as the pigeons are ready we really, really must collect the Cup because there are only ten days left till Founder's Day. Meanwhile we will concentrate on Hard Sums and Running. Strictly according to the timetable.' She looked at her tiny gold watch. 'Starting in five minutes, with Hard Sums.'

'Hooray!' cried Onyx.

After Miss Davies had gone, Owen and Onyx bustled about filling their pencil cases. Rosetti stayed at his desk, watching a large spider in its web. It reminded him of Dr Cosm. But with another part of his mind he was thinking timetable. Table. Time.

Funny.

Why did the word sound so important?

Then the bell rang, and boots roared in the corridors, and it was business as usual at Abbot Dagger's.

Next morning in the Library the Librarian found a parcel on his desk. He unwrapped it feverishly, but not feverishly enough to raise any dust. Inside it was a gold inhaler for his asthma. *From a Wellwisher*, said the card.

'Oo!' said the Librarian, hugging himself. 'How *kind*!'

For the writing on the card, thin and spidery, was the writing of Dr Cosm, who would any day now be Ruler of the Universe and Headmaster of the Academy.

Next day at lunch, Owen and Rosetti were sitting together as usual. Owen had just handed in the Hard Sums part of the Greyte Cup work, and was tucking in with the sense of a good job well done. A shadow fell over Rosetti's sausage and mash. He looked up and saw Dr Cosm, looming. 'Gnah,' said Cosm, surveying the boys with what Rosetti thought was a look of smug satisfaction. 'Do you know, insects, I think you are not getting enough sss *exercise.*'

'He's running twenty-five miles a day,' said Owen.

'So,' said Cosm, ignoring him, 'I shall expect you both on Big Side at half past two in full Footer gear. We are two short in the Victims.'

'But –'

'Otherwise,' said Cosm, 'I shall assume that you are ill, and you will be put to bed in the Sanatorium for the next two weeks. The Maximum Security wing,' he said. 'Founder's Day in mere days. You won't want to miss Founder's Day or the Greyte Cup run, nyhaha. Well?'

'Footer it is,' said Rosetti. Cosm crunched off. 'It can't be *that* bad,' said Rosetti.

'Oh yes it can,' said Slee, cracking his huge red knuckles at the next table.

'Worse,' said Damage.

'Hur, hur,' said Slee and Damage together.

The Rules of Footbrawl, Footer for short, are pretty straightforward. Basically there are two Goals and a Brawl, which is a heavy-duty sack loosely filled with gravel. The object of the game is to get the sack into your opponent's goal. Each team should be roughly the size of a Standard Class, which for the purposes of Skool Footer is reckoned to be thirty.

Abbot Dagger's Academy had a proud Footer record. Its Footerers were hand-picked from the roughest, toughest and thickest pupils. The problem, of course, was training: the Footerers could scarcely ever find anyone to compete against, because the Skolars were too clever for them and the Skoolies just ran away. Mostly, Footer trainers fixed this by dividing the classes in half, and playing the game known as Half Footer, roughly fifteen a side. But in the run-up to a big game like the Old Boys' Bloodbath on Founder's Day, the whole Footer side needed to practise as one. So, during the run-ups, Footer trainers picked scratch sides to oppose the Footer Skoolies. The scratch sides were known as Victims. Trial Games were reckoned to be good training for Teams and San staff, who got valuable experience of caring for trample injuries. The Victims . . . well, nobody worried much about the Victims.

Rosetti and Owen stood in a field of mud heavily

marked with boot studs. They were shivering. Partly this was because the usual fine rain was falling on their heads. And partly it was because they and the twenty-three smallish, thinnish, fattish or just weakish people on the Victim side were gazing drop-jawed at a thing like a cliff. Except that it was not a cliff. It was seven years' worth of Footer Skoolies, four per year, stretching from one side of the field to the other.

The ref took a deep bref.

PHEEP, went the whistle.

'CHAARGE,' cried the Footer Skoolies.

'EEK,' wailed the Victims, except Rosetti and Owen, who watched narrow-eyed, selecting their target . . .

And finding him.

He was a huge red mass of legs and face, lumbering towards them with a hungry grin. But Rosetti and Owen had travelled together through a total of thousands of years, so their teamwork was excellent.

Rosetti said to the giant, 'You have a face like a squished tomato and you smell like a hyena's bottom,' and made a childish but rude gesture.

The giant accelerated, now half-blind with rage. So he did not see Owen, on his hands and knees in his path.

'Oof!' cried the giant, tripping and falling flat on his face.

'Freedooom!' cried Rosetti, streaking through the gap in the line left by the fallen foe.

'Freedooom!' cried Owen, leaping and streaking after him.

They ran, and did not stop running. Behind them the Footer Field was a bedlam of thuds and crashes and the shrieks of the trampled. They burst into the Skolary, to find Miss Davies at the desk and Onyx beside her, pogoing with excitement.

'Boys!' cried Miss Davies. 'How lovely to – Yes? Can I help you?'

For Dr Cosm's assistant, Otto, stood framed in the doorway. 'They fled the Field of Play,' he said. 'They must return.'

'As Victims?' said Miss Davies, in a voice with a bad smell under its nose.

'Footer needs Victims,' said Otto. 'It is the Law of Nature.'

'Oh for goodness' sake go away,' said Miss Davies. 'Go on, run.' Otto left. Miss Davies put her palms together. 'Now. Onyx has found the Cup again! And as soon as the doves are ready, off we go!'

'When?'

'The day after tomorrow.'

'Which is exactly a week till Founder's Day,' said Rosetti.

'Well, we will do our best,' said Miss Davies. 'And now, Onyx will tell us where we are going, and when. Onyx?'

'Ladies and gentlemen,' said Onyx, vibrating with excitement, 'do you remember that Keeper in Rome? How he spoke jolly interestingly of lost Atlantis, birthplace of our Cup? Well, I have analysed the style of its making, and I have decided he was right! So we know for certain it was there and we'll get it for sure because nobody Dr Cosm knows is a really brilliant researcher like me!'

'If we don't, we're in trouble,' said Rosetti.

'And so is the Universe,' said Owen.

'And so is the Headmaster!' said Onyx. 'Sel*fish*! Anyway! They'll never find it! Unless they follow us! And how would they do that?'

Elsewhere in the Skool, Dr Cosm thumbed the Transmit button on his personal communicator. 'Otto!' he barked.

'Master?'

'Commence charging.'

Machinery whined. All over the Academy the lights dimmed. 'Charging.'

'Hours to full potential?'

'Twenty-three.'

'Wilco.'

And Dr Cosm strode off down the passage. The way ahead lay clear. Forward, to Universal Domination!

Eight days till Founder's Day!

8

Two days later the Skool was in a ferment. Cookery II was producing great volumes of evil brown smoke. Welding III was sticking anything it could find made of metal to anything else it could find made of metal. Year 6 Gym was bounding to and fro like kangaroos in tight white jumpsuits. Ballet XIV was staring at itself in great mirrors until it could no longer tell what was real and what was not. The Footerers demolished several granite walls with their heads out of sheer high spirits.

The staff were also affected. Dr Cosm strode to and fro in his white coat, quivering with ambition. The Headmaster made encouraging remarks in many languages, few of which anyone understood. Mato cheered the fracture clinic on in the San. And Wrekin Sartorius the Art Master murmured advice to the Art Crew as it painted a mural of Beauty triumphing over the Brute Creation, in which Beauty looked very like Miss Davies and the Brute Creation closely resembled Slee and Damage.

(Onyx had had an eye on Mr Sartorius. It struck her that he was rather keen on Miss Davies, in a worshipping sort of way.)

It was twilight when Miss Davies led the Skolars towards the farmyard. Nobody noticed them go.

'Everyone in?' said Miss Davies once the dovecote door had closed behind them.

'In,' said everyone. The air was heavy with tension.

'Hold tight,' said Miss Davies, and leaned on the Dove Pole.

Squawk. Flap. Nests in head.

The world was heaving up and down and from side to side, trying to buck them off. There was a noise, a great hollow booming. 'Let's have a look,' said Miss Davies in a voice perhaps a little tighter than usual. She opened the door. '*Well,*' she said, stepping outside.

The air was cold, and smelled of salt. The dovecote stood on the upper slopes of a low green hill. On top of the hill was a long mound covered in grass. The hill seemed to be the highest of a range of hills. On all sides, lower crests rolled away into the distance –

The not very far distance. Two hills away, the crests turned into islands, separated from each other by valleys through which grey torrents of sea surged and eddied.

'The water's rising!' squeaked Onyx.

'Or possibly,' said Owen, 'the land is sinking.'

'In which case,' said Rosetti, 'we should perhaps start looking for the Cup.'

'But *where?*' cried Onyx.

Rosetti's eyes narrowed. He appeared to be listening. 'It's calling,' he said. 'From the top of the hill.'

'I'll get it,' said Owen.

The Skolars walked swiftly up the hill. At the top was a level patch of turf. From the level patch rose a long, grassy mound.

'A barrow,' said Onyx.

'It's in there,' said Rosetti.

'Dangerous things, barrows,' said Miss Davies. 'Hey! Owen!'

But Owen was already walking between two rows of white stones to a door in the green side of the mound.

'How will it open?' said Onyx.

'Automatically,' said Miss Davies grimly.

Owen came to the stone doors and stood for a moment. There was a roar. The doors burst inwards. Owen trotted in.

He ran down a dark tunnel that turned left, then right, and got absolutely pitch-black. He ran with his arms out so he could feel the walls on either side of him, dry and lined with stone. Ahead of him was a faint glow. Towards the glow he went, one hand on each wall. There were things that felt like spiders' webs in his head, and little voices in his ears that said things like Go Back and Get From Here and What Do You Think You Are Doing. But Owen knew there were no spiders in his head and no earphones in his ears and that these things were therefore not real and therefore not worth bothering about. So he pressed on round the corner from which the light was glowing.

And came into a place that even he realized was pretty peculiar.

In front of him was a long stone box with a lid. At the far end of the box was a cube of granite. On the cube of granite stood the Greyte Cup for Achievement, glowing with a soft golden lustre.

Owen stepped on to the lid of the stone box and walked across it. He put his hand near the Cup to check if the reason for its glow was that it was hot. It seemed coolish. So he picked it up and walked back over the box.

The lid of the box moved under his feet – not a rocking movement, but a definite forward slide. Owen took two steps and jumped down. He heard the lid clonk on the stone floor behind him. He looked round. The box was open, and a figure was sitting up in it, a creature of bones without eyes dressed in armour that glowed pale blue.

'Forth!' cried the figure, pointing. 'Take the Cup from this Drowning World to its Destiny!'

Owen naturally wished to enquire what on earth

this creature was, what had happened to its eyes and how it got its armour to glow in a place that had no electricity. He took a breath to do this. Unfortunately at that moment the roof fell in.

For a moment, he felt the usual sort of crushing and smothering feelings that roof-collapse victims probably feel but do not get round to talking about for sad but obvious reasons. Then he was surprised to feel himself being shot along a tunnel in the same way that a pea is shot along a peashooter. And since Owen was not actually capable of being surprised, his brain shut down.

'Nooo!' cried Rosetti, horrorstruck as the barrow dimpled and collapsed.

'Yess!' cried Onyx, clapping her hands.

For the doorway of the barrow bulged like a pair of lips and said *PTOOOOARR*, halfway between a spit and a roar. And out of the door shot Owen like a bullet from a gun. He hit the ground, turned two somersaults and landed on his feet.

He shook his head. Soil flew out of his hair. His face wore its first ever dazed expression.

'Look!' cried Onyx. '*Look!*'

Rosetti looked. Miss Davies looked. A mammoth on the next hill paused in its trumpeting and looked.

In Owen's hands, glowing golden in the sun, was the Greyte Cup.

'Right!' cried Miss Davies. 'Everyone back to the dovecote, quick!'

Everyone started to run towards the dovecote. The ground was shaking, the sound of the rising sea a sluicing roar. Then above the roar of the sea came a new noise – a clanking and a bellowing that sounded like a Footer cheer, though of course that could not be right, because this was the sinking of Atlantis and Footer would not be invented for thousands of –

Over the horizon there galloped two very large people. They paused, looking around.

'Slee,' said Rosetti. 'Damage. Run, Owen!'

Owen turned to run. His feet got mixed up with each other. The Footbrawlers charged him down. Slee stooped and plucked the Cup out of his hands. The two of them ran on towards the dovecote.

Rosetti ran to head them off. The Footerers knocked him down. Then they piled into the dovecote and slammed the door.

'No!' said Miss Davies.

The dovecote door opened again. A figure sailed out and landed face first in the grass. The door closed.

The dovecote vanished like a blown-out flame.

The Polymathic Skolars stood open-mouthed, abandoned on a hillside in drowning Atlantis.

The face-down figure got up and groaned. It was wearing the remains of a beautiful tweed suit.

Flicking an artistic forelock out of its eye, it said, 'What place is this?'

'Wrekin!' cried Miss Davies, her eyes lighting up.

Wrekin Sartorius looked around him. Then he said, 'The tide seems to be coming in. Top of the hill?'

To the top of the hill they went, slowly, the way people would walk if they had recently been struck by lightning.

'Well,' said Miss Davies, when they reached the ruins of the burial mound. 'Here we are.'

All around them, great waves were crashing in on the sinking land.

'Wild and splendid calamity,' murmured Wrekin Sartorius. 'What happened?'

'Dr Cosm came back here in his Time Machine,' said Owen. 'He brought Slee and Damage. They stole the Greyte Cup and now they have stolen our Time Machine. So they have won the Grail and we're stuck.'

'And it's getting a bit crowded up here,' said Onyx. There were indeed animals everywhere on the remaining bump of dry land. Rosetti had the faraway look in his eye that meant he was speaking to non-human creatures with his mind. Onyx found she was holding Miss Davies's hand.

'Shoo,' said Owen, batting away a sabre-toothed cat that was trying to climb on to his head.

'And if I might ask,' said Miss Davies, 'what exactly are you doing here, Wrekin?'

'I stowed away,' said Sartorius.

'Why?'

'I have been watching you. I had an inkling of Cosm's plotting, and I think he is dangerous. I wanted . . . to protect . . . you,' said Sartorius, going scarlet and avoiding Miss Davies's eye.

'Some hope,' said Miss Davies, blushing herself.

'And I must say,' said Wrekin, 'that although the protecting part has not worked out very well, I am happy, nay honoured, to be –'

'Excuse me,' said Rosetti, 'this is all very interesting but by my reckoning in ten minutes Atlantis will be one hundred per cent sunk.' He moved to avoid being trodden on by a woolly rhinoceros. 'And these animals are hostile when frightened and I am having trouble keeping them calm.'

'True,' said Miss Davies.

'So what shall we do?'

Miss Davies closed her eyes. 'Father,' she said.

A huge wave reared a vast grey head, hung over the land and burst white upon the grassy slope. The ground shook. A blast of salt spray rolled over the people and animals, who squealed and roared with terror, according to species. And remarkable species they were.

'Look!' said Owen, fascinated. 'A direwolf, ancestor of both the domestic dog and the woewolf.'

'Behind you, Onyx,' hissed Rosetti.

Onyx turned. A direwolf was crouching, ready to spring. It measured two metres to the shoulder

'Help!' cried Onyx.

'I can't get through to its mind,' said Rosetti. 'Too primitive.'

'Ye anymall bee quyte anciente alsoe,' said a creaking voice behind him. 'Ha ha. Begone, creature.'

The direwolf's eyes crossed, and it leaped into the sea. Abbott Dagger (for it was he) bowed deeply, sweeping the ground with his hat feather. 'You called, deare Daughter,' he said. 'I begge ye, enter my Cabine of Voyagyng.' He led them over the horizon and indicated the odd contrivance resting on the ground there. It looked like a flat-bottomed ship, with windows all round it. 'Yn ye Clymbe.'

'Father!' said Miss Davies.

'I knowe, ye Cupp, disaster, but Layterr. For lo, ye waters ryse –'

'*Father!* Oh dear, too late,' sighed Miss Davies.

'Too layte? Saye, rather, too earlye,' said Abbott Dagger, chortling at his great wit.

'Thou haste trod in ye accident of ye direwolfe,' said his daughter.

'Blaste, blaste, *blaste*!' cried the Abbot, wiping his shoe on one of the few tufts of grass remaining above water in Atlantis.

'Ahem,' said Rosetti. 'I think perhaps we ought to be, er . . .'

'Zooks!' cried the Abbot, for the Time Ship was now floating on water, and beating against the hilltop with every wave that arrived. 'Yn!'

In they all leaped. The smell of direwolf accident was strong, but the desire to escape was stronger. The last thing Onyx saw as the door closed was the sea full of animals swimming towards the distant line of what must have been the mainland . . .

Squawk, flap, nests in head. The door opened again.

'Home Time,' said the Abbot. 'Out with ye! Begone!'

The children found themselves standing in the dark and ruined farmyard. Miss Davies waved. The Time Ship went out like a candle flame.

'Ah,' said Miss Davies, walking across the yard. 'I see they brought back the dovecote.' She stuck her head in at the door. 'Looks all right. But how did they get there?'

'The Time Table,' said Rosetti.

'The wha?'

'I realized when you were talking the other day. We saw it when we were in the Duggan Cube that night. I thought it was furniture but it was a machine. It looks like a grey metal table with chairs round it.'

Miss Davies sat down on a stone. 'So you were

right,' she said. 'I . . . well, I suppose I have foolishly been too proud to admit it. A terrible fault. Learn from it.' She shook her head, while the Skolars made soothing noises. 'I just couldn't believe that anyone would be so *irresponsible*. Have they considered the doom they may bring on the universe? It is bad. Very, very bad. Sorry, Skolars.'

'Never mind sorry,' said Rosetti. 'Look.' The Skool lights flickered. They became dimmer, and stayed that way.

'They're charging something up,' said Rosetti. 'And we know what it is.'

'They don't need to go Time Travelling any more,' said Miss Davies, despondent. 'They've got the Cup. We are all doomed.'

'Not yet. They won't have brought it back,' said Rosetti. 'They know it Calls me. So they will have hidden it in Time again. They must have gone straight from Atlantis to . . . wherever.' He frowned. 'I've been hearing it lately, even far away in Time. But it's gone now. I think it's in the Far Past, before it was made.'

'Can they do that?'

'Like you said, obviously,' said Owen. 'If they hid it somewhere deep and quiet where it didn't change anything important.'

'So where?'

'Don't know.'

'There are still six days to Founder's Day,' said Owen. 'Enough for one more trip. That's all.'

'I know,' said Onyx. 'I'll read a book.'

'Reading is a waste of –'

'Reading is never a waste of anything,' said Miss Davies hastily. 'Now I will lock up this dovecote and we will have tea and make a plan.'

'Locking won't be enough,' said Rosetti. 'We need a trap.'

'I am not losing anyone in Time,' said Miss Davies. 'Not even meatheads.'

'Who said anything about Time?' said Rosetti.

'What, then?'

'A Blastoff Doorstep.'

'Heh heh,' said Owen, who was getting the hang of this laughing business.

'Whatever,' said Miss Davies, shaking her head despairingly.

Onyx and Miss Davies cooked sausages in the black iron pan over the Study fire. As the final banger banged, Rosetti and Owen came in, looking evil but happy.

'Well,' said Miss Davies. 'Did you manage the dovecote surprise?'

'Yep,' said Owen. 'Do the bad guys know we're back yet?'

'I don't think so,' said Miss Davies.

'They will,' said Rosetti.

*

Dr Cosm was in his office ruling red-ink lines on his plan for World Domination when he heard a tiny scratching on the door. 'Enter!' he cried.

The door opened a crack. Otto's minute head appeared. 'O Great One,' he said –

'Call me Headmaster-Designate,' said Dr Cosm. 'Or HMD.'

'Er, HMD. They're back.'

'Who are back?'

'You know who. From you know where.'

'*What?*' cried Cosm, his currant eyes vanishing in mean white folds of suet.

'True, HMD.'

Cosm crushed an exquisite china Head of Einstein in his slimy hand. 'Sss,' he said. 'I would have thought it impossible, hmm. Well, from now on, it is No More Mister Nice Guy.'

'It wasn't particularly nice to maroon them in Atlantis,' said Otto.

'Shut up! Meddling insects!' There was white foam on the white chin. 'They think they have foiled me! Well, I shall make sure that they never travel the years again! Nyahaha!'

'Nya–'

'Shut up!' cried Cosm. 'Fetch me my faithful brutes Slee and Damage!'

'Coming up, master!' cried Otto, and scuttled away.

'We see how they travel in a dovecote with no

roof and no walls and graffiti all over it,' hissed Cosm through a rising billow of foam. A battering came on the door. 'Enter, my thickheaded beauties, and listen to your master!'

'Yeah,' said Slee, entering.

'Orright,' said Damage, doing the same.

'See how they obey me!' hissed Cosm foamily. 'Now, apes. Here are your instructions. Listen up, and keep listening!'

Damage and Slee were well naffed off that the Poly Skolars were back. Dr Cosm had said their Time Machine was dead primitive and needed wrecking because of health and safety. As far as Damage and Slee were concerned primitive was just another long word they did not understand and health and safety were two more but shorter. They understood wrecking, though. So along to the barnyard they stomped.

The dovecote looked small and half-wrecked already under the narrow moon. Slee pushed the door. ''S locked,' he said.

'I'll kick 'im in,' said Damage.

'Me too,' said Slee, anxious not to be left out.

'Formation double Brawlboot. One.'

'Two,' said Damage.

'Fa-REE,' they said together, and put the boot in.

Which explains why what happened next happened to both of them.

The boots hit the door. Inside the door, an electric contact touched another electric contact, completing a circuit that shot a spark into a small charge of nitroglycerine placed by thoughtful Owen under the flagstone in front of the dovecote's door. The flagstone leaped into the air. Damage and Slee went with it, arcing across the barnyard and through a hole Rosetti had made in the roof of the cowshed.

The ex-cowshed. The now empty-space-shed. The not-quite-empty-space-shed.

When Rosetti had listened with his mind for living creatures hereabouts, he had heard many small, thirsty voices. While Owen had been wiring up the Blastoff Doorstep, Rosetti had called in a tiny, gentle voice. And the owners of the little voices had hopped and hopped, until they were waiting under the hole in the roof. They made quite a crowd. Actually, there were so many of them that they were more like a pile than a crowd.

'Yum, yum,' said a million tiny voices.

And here come Damage and Slee, scorched and plummeting.

'AIEE,' cried Slee, hurtling through the hole and landing with a bump.

'AROOO,' cried Damage, doing roughly the same thing.

'Lucky,' said Damage, flat on his back on the floor.

'*Well* lucky,' said Slee, also flat.

'Yum, yum,' said the tiny voices, hopping towards the large, juicy bodies and climbing aboard. 'We have not eaten for two years and you guys are the greatest packed lunch we have ever seen.'

'Eek!' cried Slee.

'*Fleas!*' cried Damage.

And the two Footerers ran scratching back to their study. Which to a few thousand fleas looked like the biggest and most wonderfully stocked picnic site in the world, ever.

At roughly the same time as all this was happening, a Governors' Meeting was taking place.

'So,' said the Headmaster, reading from his notes. 'Founder's Day. I presume that all is in order?'

'What passes for it around here,' said Dr Cosm.

'And by the way,' said Commissioner Manacle. 'We are sure that nothing has . . . *happened* to the Greyte Cup, are we?'

The Head met the Commissioner's piercing glare with his own vague, kindly one. 'Oh, quite,' he said.

'Because if for any reason it is not there,' said Manacle, 'it will definitely be the moment for Dr Cosm to take over.'

'Ha!' said the Head, with a hollow chuckle. 'Laughable!'

But it looked to Commissioner Manacle as if inside the Head was not laughing. Not even a tiny bit.

Three days before Founder's Day the Quest for the Holy Grail was important, but not as important as the sports. Owen made a large hole in the Long Jump pit and was treated for mild concussion. Onyx missed the Vaulting Horse and had to be brought down from the gym ceiling by a man with a ladder. And at three o'clock Rosetti was jogging on the start line of the Cross-country Running course.

'Right,' said Dr Cosm to Slee and Damage, at the other end of the start line. 'Your instructions.'

'Rr,' said Slee, scratching.

'Pesky fleas,' said Damage, scratching too.

'I want you to nobble Svenson,' said Cosm. 'Stop scratching, will you?'

'On your marks!' cried the starter. 'Go!'

Rosetti went. So did the rest of the field, except Slee and Damage, who were too busy scratching.

'Oh,' said Slee, breaking into a run. 'How we going to do the nobbling, then?'

'From behind?' said Damage, peering over the horizon in front of them.

Off they went.

*

'Well done!' cried the Skolars and Miss Davies and the Head as Rosetti cantered over the finish line an hour and a half later. The runner up was ten minutes behind him. There was no sign of Slee and Damage. 'Any trouble?'

'Trouble?' said Rosetti. 'No. Why?'

When Rosetti was on his way to tea, Slee tripped him up and Damage sat on him. 'You're nobbled,' they said, scratching.

'Sss,' said Dr Cosm, in front of his screens. 'Too late, morons!'

'I hear that Keene's Lovely Writing is brilliant, and French's Hard Sums are a work of positive genius, and now Svenson has won the Cross-country,' said Otto. 'I hate to say this, Doctor, but I think the Skolars have the Cup in the bag. Curse them, obviously,' he added hastily.

'Hah!' cried Cosm scornfully. 'To win a Cup you need a Cup. And they have no Cup, nyhaha.'

'Nyaha,' said Otto nervously.

'Shut *up*,' said Cosm.

The day after the Cross-country, two days before Founder's Day, a Security Master with a cattle prod and loudhailer stumped through the Hall of Session after lunch. 'All will report to Big Side to watch the Old Boys' Bloodbath and cheer a lot,' he cried.

The Skolars trudged over to Big Side.

'Oo! Team!' cried Onyx, bouncing. 'Skool-a-SKOOL!'

'I think you're mad,' said Rosetti. 'They tried to maroon us in Atlantis.'

'And they keep pinching the Cup, and they've hidden it somewhen else,' said Owen. 'And they've got fleas and they want to destroy the Universe.'

'Oh, *well*!' said Onyx. 'But just *look* at them! SKOOL!'

The Skool Team was indeed impressive. The Old Boys were huge, but they looked as if they ate too many pies and watched too much TV. The Skool Team looked as if they ate live wildcats instead of pies and did press-ups instead of watching TV.

'CHAARGE!' roared a voice. The Skool Team thundered down on the Old Boys. The Skool Team went *THUD*. The Old Boys went *SPLAT*. The pile of giants rolled yelling and battering towards the goal.

'Wow,' said Onyx. Then she noticed that Elphine the Match Girl was standing next to her. Elphine looked rather sulky. 'Something wrong?' said Onyx.

'Slee,' said Elphine, scratching.

'What about him?'

'He got blown up. And fleas after.'

'Oh *dear*,' said Onyx, trying to sound sincere but not managing.

'He's a idiot,' said Elphine, rolling her eyes away from Slee, who was running across the field with the ball under his arm. 'I don't fancy him no more. Getting blowed up. Pafetic. I fancy people who *do* the blowing up. Not *get* blowed up. And give you fleas after.'

'Oo,' said Onyx. 'We did it.'

Elphine turned, a worshipping light in her eye. 'You *did*? *Brilliant!*'

Onyx was rather pleased. She had never been liked by anyone as tough as Elphine before. She had a sudden inspiration. The Cup would be deeply hidden; perhaps too deep for libraries to reveal its whereabouts. What would Rosetti have done? Something crafty, obviously. Perhaps this was a time for . . . *cunning*.

'What we were wondering,' said Onyx, trying to keep down the urge to tee hee keenly, 'was whether silly old Slee said anything about going away on a, well, a holiday or something? Probably to biff people?'

'Oh. Yeah. He's off to a cave,' said Elphine. 'Called Lazy Daisy or somefink.' She lit a match in a faraway manner. 'Explosions,' she said. 'Cool!'

Simple as that, thought Onyx, and scuttled off.

9

'Deep underground,' said Onyx. 'Deep, deep, deep, *deep –*'

'What are you talking about?' said Owen.

'Start at the beginning, Onyx, dear,' murmured Miss Davies.

'*Well*,' said Onyx through a red mist, for she was so excited that she kept forgetting to breathe. 'Elphine said Slee was off to caves and Lazy Daisy. So I asked the Head, and he said he couldn't remember, but paintings came into it. And then I asked Mr Sartorius, and he gave me this.'

Her fellow Skolars peered at the book in her hands. There were pictures of bison charging, horses dancing, little stick men with spears. Owen said, 'What is it?'

'Cave paintings,' said Rosetti. 'At Les Eyzies. In France.'

'Which to someone as stupid as Slee sounds like Lazy Daisy,' said Onyx in an annoying voice. 'So I think the Cosm people have hidden the Cup in the caves and we absolutely must go back in time and get it because tomorrow is Founder's Day and we cannot let Dr Cosm be Headmaster and probably destroy the Universe because it would just be too awful.'

'Quite,' said Rosetti.

'Good research,' said Owen.

Miss Davies's brows came down over her fierce gold eyes. 'The pigeons will be ready by teatime. See you in the farmyard after tea. Bring outdoor gear and torches.'

'Yes, Miss Davies,' said everyone. But Rosetti got the impression that she thought this was a last throw. And that she was not very confident they were going to win.

After tea, everyone trooped down to the farmyard with their equipment (Rosetti had packed a cricket stump, just in case). Miss Davies was already there. Into the dovecote they marched, and squeezed into the chair. As Miss Davies raised the Nudging Pole, there was a knock on the door.

'Er . . .' said a voice.

'*Wrekin!*' cried Miss Davies, going pink.

'There's no room,' said Owen, who did not hold with artists.

'He can sit on my knee,' said Miss Davies.

'Ik,' said Rosetti.

Flap. Squawk. Nests in the mind.

It was cold: a thin cold that rode through the door-cracks on the breeze, penetrated anorak and found bone. The dovecote was on a limestony hillside covered in scrub. The air was dry, and so was the ground.

'Look!' said Rosetti, pointing.

Along the bottom of the hill wound a river full of grey-blue water. In the distance a blue-white blanket lay across the world.

'How interesting. That must be the Massif Central ice,' said Owen.

Rosetti cocked his head, listening to something the others could not hear. 'It's here. It's calling. From below. Look for holes. Caves.'

They scrambled through the scrub, glad of having something to do in the cold.

'Nothing,' said Owen.

'Nothing,' said Rosetti.

There was a crash.

'Ouch!' said the voice of Onyx.

Rosetti and Owen trampled their way through the scrub towards her voice. They saw Onyx's legs sticking out of what looked like a collapsed badger sett.

Rosetti pulled her out and wriggled down the hole. 'It opens out,' said his voice, strangely hollow. 'Come on!'

They went.

The hole started narrow and rooty and smelling

powerfully of badger. Just as Onyx thought she was going to suffocate, she felt moving air on her face and saw a light. The light became Rosetti, standing in a stone cave waving his torch. She squeezed out of the tunnel and helped Rosetti pull Owen through. In the torchlight, a narrow path wound away into the darkness between pale pillars whose tops were lost in shadow. They started down the path. The air smelled wet and stony, and everywhere was the drip of falling water. Nobody spoke.

Soon they were wading in an icy stream, still travelling downwards. They followed it for twenty minutes. Rosetti walked round a corner, took a step and found emptiness. Onyx heard a splash. When she rounded the corner she saw him struggling in a pool of water deeper than he was tall. On the right-hand side of the pool, the water flowed out through a notch, falling into empty space with a hollow booming. On the far side of the bowl, a dry tunnel pierced the rock wall.

'Over here!' cried Onyx, pointing the way with her torch. Above the mouth of the dry tunnel someone had drawn a picture of a stick man, walking.

'It's a signpost,' said Rosetti, teeth chattering.

The dry tunnel was floored with gravel. It opened into a wide gallery. In an alcove off the gallery was a pile of furs.

'There are people down here,' said Rosetti,

wrapping himself in a skin that by the smell of it had once belonged to a bear.

'They'll be awfully pleased to see us,' said Onyx.

'No,' said Owen. 'These are very basic people. They will think that anyone down here is either a predator or a rival tribe.'

'Gulp,' said Onyx.

'Look!' said Rosetti, shining his torch on the wall.

Across the grey rock there leaped an animal, bright red and yellow: a deer, full of life and energy.

'It could have been painted yesterday,' said Rosetti.

'It probably was,' said Owen.

This was a bit of a conversation stopper. Not that anything could stop Onyx. 'I recognize this from the books,' she said. 'We go on down here, and there's a right turning and there's a big hall at the far end with a lot of paintings –'

'AROO,' cried a voice deep in the tunnels.

Rosetti yanked his two companions back into an alcove in the passage. 'Lights *out*!' he hissed.

Just in time. Feet were running towards them out of the inky dark; feet small and bare, running two-footed like human beings but with the lightness of animals.

The little feet fluttered past, pit-a-pat. Behind them came a heavier pounding.

Footbrawl boots.

'AHEEEE,' cried a voice.

'HUR HUR,' cried another.

The boots went past. Something clattered.

The boots died away. There was only silence, thick and dark, with the drip of water.

Rosetti turned on his torch.

There were footprints in a patch of sand; little footprints, with widely spread toes. But not little enough to blot out the bigger footprints of the people they had been chasing. The bigger fooprints had dents in them. The marks of Footer boot studs.

'Look!' said Onyx, stooping to pick something up. The thing that had made the clatter was an arrow. 'It's lovely,' said Onyx.

It had a head of chipped flint, razor sharp, bound to a shaft of peeled stick with a lashing of sinew dyed red, fletched with something that Onyx instantly identified as the wing feathers of the Great Bustard. Onyx and Rosetti gazed upon it in rapture.

'Ahem,' said Owen.

'Wha.'

'What about the Cup?'

Then everyone froze. For a terrible moaning slithered out of the darkness. 'OOOO,' it went.

'Could be a cave bear,' said Onyx. 'Stands twelve foot to the shoulder.'

'Teeth like huge great knife blades,' said Rosetti.

'Ulp,' said Owen.

'OOOO,' said the voice again, bestial, agonized. Strangely . . . *muffled.*

'It's not an animal,' said Rosetti.

'OOO,' cried the Not Animal. 'WOOOOE IS MEEE. I AM UNDONE, LACKADAY LACKADAY.'

'A person,' said Rosetti.

'An Elizabethan person,' said Onyx.

They moved out into the tunnel. The beams of the torches swept over painted herds of deer and bears and aurochs and crowds of little running men with spears and darts.

'Let's *look!*' cried Onyx.

'Let's get after them!' said Owen. 'If we don't hurry, the Universe ends.'

'I think we've lost them anyway,' said Onyx. 'There's someone in trouble in here. Let's help!'

The Skolars' feet rang hollow and echoing, and their torch beams stabbed into an enormous vault. They stood in the middle of the floor, their torches making a little puddle of light in a vast dome of darkness. They turned slowly round, together – it seemed important to stay together, far underground, thirty thousand years from home. They walked slowly towards the wall –

'Eek!' cried Onyx.

They were looking at a tiger. It had vast yellow

eyes and a red cave of a mouth. Onyx found she had got behind Rosetti, who found he had got behind Owen. Owen had not moved. Actually he seemed to be . . . yawning.

'Don't make it cross,' hissed Rosetti.

'Funny how seeing things with their mouths open makes you want to yawn,' said Owen.

'*Owen!*' hissed Rosetti.

'It's only a picture,' said Owen.

'Oh,' said Onyx, braver.

'Ah,' said Rosetti, ashamed. 'And look.'

Below the tiger's paws was a painting of something yellow.

The Greyte Cup.

'It was here,' said Rosetti.

'And now they've taken it somewhere else,' said Onyx.

'Ooooh,' moaned something in the dark.

Three heads snapped round. Three torch beams followed the heads.

It was a person. A person sitting against the wall with its head in its hands. A person who lifted up his head without taking his hands away from his eyes. A person who even though he still had his hands over his eyes was looking at them. Not with a real eye, they noticed, but an eye *tattooed* in the middle of his forehead.

'Trym!' cried Rosetti. 'What are you doing here?'

'UWWWWW,' moaned the Mage's Assistant and Dovemaster, for it was he. 'NOE! SPARE MEE, O LOVELY PEOPLE, WITH YOUR BOWS AND ARROES AND YOUR TEENY FEET! TAKE SLEE AND DAMAGE, THEY BEE STOUTER AND MORE MEATIE. Oh, ytt is ye, Rosetti. My lippes are sealed.'

'Fine,' said Rosetti. 'We'll be off, then. The little people with the arrows will be back any minute.'

'Noe,' said Trym in a small voice. 'I was not borne for Sacrifyce. The tiny folke with the Arroes wyll returne and make mee a Sacrifyce to the Tyger. I was promised to them by ye Doctor, ere he took the Cupp from where he had Hyd it, hymme and hys Thugges.'

'The Doctor?'

'Cosm. He ys in ye Caves, Hymselfe. He took the Cupp. Then he struck me and I was mazed. Then he ran away. Ye lyttle people chased hymme.'

'*Well!*' cried Onyx, shocked.

'Tell us,' said Rosetti. 'What has been happening?'

'Wylt thou take mee hence?'

'We'll think about it. Tell.'

'Alle ryghte,' said Trym. 'Heere Goes. Ytt was ye faulte of –'

'Excuse me,' said Owen, 'but please talk properly.'

'Oh all *right*!' said Trym. 'Well how was I supposed to know he wanted to conquer the *Universe*?'

'Wha,' said Owen.

'Who?' said Onyx.

'Start at the beginning,' said Rosetti.

'Not till we're out of here,' said Trym.

'All right.'

They marched down the tunnel, crossed the sinkhole, splashed through the icy water of the stream to the bottom of the badger sett and squeezed into the thin, chilly breeze of the Ice Age. The light was horribly bright. The dovecote was still there. A couple of arrows stuck out of the walls. Miss Davies and Wrekin Sartorius were sitting on a bench by the door, holding hands and soaking up the chilly sun.

'*There* you are,' said Miss Davies with her beautiful smile. 'All these Cave People rushed out chasing Slee and Damage and Cosm. We did so hope you were all right, and that you'd got the Cup.'

'How did you get *rid* of the Cave People?' said Onyx.

'Wrekin painted them. They started to worship him and he sent them away. Where's the Cup?'

'Cosm's got it.'

'Oh dear,' said Miss Davies.

'And Trym is about to tell us what is going on,' said Onyx.

'I have been so blind. I blame myself,' said Miss Davies. 'And at the same time I am very, very furious.' Her golden eyes had an angry, reddish light. 'Come on, then, Trym. Spit it out or we'll leave you behind to be chopped up with little flint knives.'

'But the honourable lovely cultured children said –'

'Come *on*!' cried Miss Davies in a terrible voice.

'Ooer!' said Trym. 'Well. Your father the Abbot is crool hard on me. I am the greatest Dovemaster the world has ever known. But it was always Feed those doves, Trym, Mop that up, Trym, Get this chamber pot off me foot, Trym, and never mind the stink. Well, I was doing all the work and he was the Great Mage, famous, revered by all. So I was looking for a way to take my master's place and earn big money. And there came to the House of Dagger a Queen's man of stern mind and no humour, a tax collector, one Abanazar Cosm –'

'A *tax* collector?' said Miss Davies.

'Aye. And when your father heard Cosm was searching for his goods so he could take them for the Queen, he hid them. And Cosm offered me money to find the Cup where your father had hid it in Time. And I agreed, and told him of the Sealed Room. Anyone would have.'

'Anyone with the soul of a worm,' said Miss Davies.

'Worms have their uses,' said Owen.

'Well,' said Trym. 'Abanazar Cosm was kind to me, unlike the Abbot. He took me at my true worth, and treated me as an equal. So I took him some doves. And he by cunning art did make a copy of their minds, that he used as an engine for his device that he called a Time Table.'

'See?' said Owen.

'If you have quite finished,' said Trym huffily. 'Anyway. With this Time Table we did travel in Time, first stealing the Cup from its Sealed Room. By now Cosm had learned from me that the Cup was the Grail, and he liked your Home Time, particularly the anaesthetics and the dentists and the loose clothes. He forgot his vows to the Queen, and decided to work for himself, not her. And now he plans to use the Cup to dominate the Universe. And as you went to take it from the deeps of Time, so the Doctor took it ten minutes ahead of you, using as his soldiers two oafs called Duggan. And hid it each time further back in Time. He hath promised me Power and a Kingdom when he shall rule the Universe. Because I am worth it.'

'All this we had already divined, except the last, which is balderdash,' said Miss Davies, with a sniff. 'And what we yet wish to know, so you can perhaps save yourself from being sacrificed by these small cross people, is to tell us where Dr Cosm has gone now.'

'To hide the Cup in the Past yet further, sixty-five million years before Founder's Day exactly, they said, before they struck my head and tyed me up and left me for Sacrifyce, curse them, traitors, dogs.'

'I can hear it,' said Rosetti. 'Faint and far away. But definitely there.'

'Dear me,' said Miss Davies. 'Well, we had better go and find it. I wonder if the doves will make it.'

'Two trips in a day?' said Owen.

'We may be lucky,' said Miss Davies. 'Granted, that's two trips on one recharge. But we have the greatest Dovemaster in the world with us.' (Here she smiled flatteringly at Trym.) 'Anyway, it's a risk we have to take. If they open the chamber and find it empty in front of the whole Skool, the world will change and the Dread Thing will happen. Fingers crossed, everyone.'

Everyone climbed in and squeezed into the chair. Miss Davies prodded the basket with the pole.

Flap. Squawk. Nests in head.

Suddenly everyone was coughing.

'It's *hot*!' said Onyx.

It was. The air was thick and wet and smelled like a compost heap. There was a buzzing and a humming outside. Something huge bumped into something solid and walked off with a step that made the ground shake. Miss Davies peered into the dove basket. The birds were lying on the bottom, unmoving.

'Are they dead?' said Owen.

'Trym?' said Miss Davies.

Trym sucked his teeth. 'Not dead. Only sleeping.'

'Good,' said Owen.

'Good if they wake up,' said Miss Davies. 'Open the door, somebody.'

Outside, something roared.

Rosetti said, 'You sure?'

'No open door, no get Cup,' said Onyx. 'Ooer.'

For Owen had already done the job, and stepped out.

Into a rather alarming place.

The dovecote was in a little grove of trees, except that they were not trees, but things that looked like ferns with stalks.

'Cycads!' said Onyx.

'Owen! Duck!' cried Miss Davies.

Owen ducked. A dragonfly came droning through the branches: a dragonfly with wings two metres from tip to tip and jaws that clashed together where Owen's head would have been, spraying him with greenish spit. Beyond the grove was a cone-topped mountain, leaking smoke from its summit.

Rosetti said, 'Something's weird.'

Onyx said, 'Well it *is* the Cretaceous, silly!'

Owen said, 'Everything's got two shadows.'

Everything had. The sun was leaking through the water vapour and volcano smoke, throwing the black shadows of the fronds on the dead-leaf floor. But each leaf had a second shadow, fainter, slightly red-coloured. An orange streak shone horribly bright among the clouds.

'What's *that*?' said Rosetti.

'It's a meteor,' said Owen. 'In a decaying orbit.'

'The Chicxulub meteor,' said Onyx.

'The wha?'

'It's *so* interesting!' said Onyx. 'It wiped out the dinosaurs. An enormous –'

'A Dread Thing,' said Owen. 'How very interesting. This is what happens when you bring the Cup back into a Time when it doesn't exist and never could have and its actual presence disturbs the normal course of events.'

'So I think we should find the Cup and leave,' said Miss Davies, over a crashing in the cycads. 'I think the dinosaurs have . . . maybe twenty minutes to live. Look out!'

A greenish creature the size and general shape of a kangaroo bounded into the glade, gnashing its vast teeth.

'Help!' cried Onyx, clutching Rosetti's arm.

Miss Davies said, 'Back in the dovecote!' But as she opened her mouth, a sound came from the cycads at the end of the grove. Not a roar, this time, but a shout. Not precisely a *human* shout, but a shout as close to human as you got from Slee or Damage Duggan.

The green kangaroo thing swung its awful head towards the sound and bounded away into the trees, clashing its teeth. There was another Duggan shout and a thud, and the noise of something kangaroo-shaped and heavily battered dragging itself away through the trees.

'WE EATS DINOTHINGS FOR BRECK-FUS,' roared a Duggan voice, to the tune of John Brown's Body.

'Right,' said Rosetti, and started into the grove, swatting enormous insects with his cricket stump.

'Hey!' cried just about everybody else. Then they went after him, Onyx first, bouncing, for she felt that something amazing was going to happen.

She was right.

She found Rosetti in a little glade. He was not alone. Also in the glade were the big table and chairs of grey metal that Owen and Rosetti had last seen in the High Energy Physics Lab. Round the table sat Dr Cosm, Otto, Slee and Damage.

'Morning, all,' said Rosetti.

'Wha,' said Slee.

'Wha,' said Damage.

'Eh?' said Otto.

'Aha,' said Dr Cosm, his little black eyes glinting among their suety folds. 'The pigeon fanciers. And Trym, I see. Welcome to *real* Time Travel.' He made a sweeping gesture of his hand. 'And to the Time Table.'

Rosetti's eyes had travelled to the middle of the table, where two things stood. One was something roughly the shape of a pigeon's head, encased in glass and giving off a strange, headachy light. And the other was the Greyte Cup for Achievement, otherwise the Holy Grail. He said, 'Hand over the Cup, Abanazar Tax Boy.'

'Tax boy?' said Dr Cosm. '*Tax boy?* Nyaha.' His voice was cold as the clatter of ice cubes. 'I have changed. I have left my Tax shell, and my gorgeous wings are open. Call me rather "Master".'

'That's right, call him rather "Master",' said Otto.

'Shut up.'

'Stop bickering,' said Rosetti. 'The Cup.'

'Hah!' cried Cosm. 'In five minutes, the time will be ripe for us to return to the Skool, humiliate that fool of a Head, and bring the Cup before the Governors with our own hands. Meanwhile you will be here, and the Star will fall –'

'Excuse me,' said Onyx. She did not much like looking at Dr Cosm's bulging eyes and suety skin, so she had been concentrating on other things. In particular, she had been concentrating on a sort of shaking in the ground, as of mighty footsteps. 'But I think a Dread Thing is about to happen. Because of you altering History and all that.'

'Nonsense.'

Onyx actually found Cosm, Master of the Universe, rather frightening. 'But,' she said, 'even if you don't believe in actual Dread Things, I think, well, that is, something's *coming*.'

'Nonsense!' cried Cosm again. 'Nothing can stand in my waAAIIEEE!'

At this point, the following things happened.

1. The footsteps had got heavier and louder until the actual ground was trembling, and there was a crashing in the grove as if something enormous was marching through the branches, and Otto and the Duggans were peering dully into the double shadows.

2. The ground was shaking because of the footsteps (see above). But another shaking was starting. A tooth-rattling shaking. Bigger. *Much* bigger.

'Earthquake,' said Rosetti nervously.

'That,' said Owen, 'would be the gravitational pull of the large meteor that is about to wipe out eighty-five per cent of life on Earth for several million years, providing a fresh start for History. Which is what Dread Things do.'

'Ah,' said Rosetti, not consoled.

3. While everyone was being nervous and peering into the shadows, Trym was scowling and grinding his teeth. Suddenly he twitched the cricket stump

from Rosetti's slack hand, leaped on to the Time Table, bashed in the glass pigeon's head, scooped up the Greyte Cup, leaped off the table again and rushed to hide behind Owen. There was an explosion. A small pink mushroom cloud rose from the pigeon's head. A clock chimed four billion in many invisible places.

'NOOOO!' roared Dr Cosm.

There was a short, thick silence.

'So,' said Miss Davies. 'The Time Table is stuck in the Past. But it also exists in the Present, and it is quite big, and not at all mythical. Skolars, this may explain the things we saw in the Examinator in my father's house. Without this idiot, the Cretaceous might have gone on forever. So tell me, Taxman Abanazar Cosm, how does it feel to be the man who wiped out the dinosaurs?'

Being slow on the uptake, Slee and Damage did not get what was going on and were still gazing into the trees, where the footsteps were getting louder and had actually become a rhythmic crashing.

'Prolly a Trannysaurus,' said Slee.

'Trannysaurus Wrecked,' said Damage.

'Soon will be. Hur hur,' said Slee.

The crashing got practically deafening. Several trees fell over. Twenty metres above them, a green head the size of a bus opened a black mouth the size of a garage lined with yellow teeth the size of lamp posts.

'Ooer,' said Slee.

'Get us out of here,' said Damage.

Cosm said nothing, being busy sprinting for the trees.

'Wha,' said Slee.

'Run,' said Damage.

Down came the head. Wide gaped the mouth. Clash went the teeth, missing by inches. 'Arrghrr,' went the huge voice of *Tyrannosaurus maximperator*, the biggest meat-eater of them all (just because no fossils have shown up does not mean it never existed), as it set off in pursuit of beefy Slee and meaty Damage.

Perhaps the Duggans could have eaten *Tyrannosaurus rex* for breakfast.

But it was a definite fact that *Tyrannosaurus maximperator* could eat Duggans for breakfast.

Suddenly the clearing was full of people sprinting towards the dovecote.

Silence fell, except for the rumble of earthquakes, the roar of erupting volcanoes and the bellow of great beasts minutes from extinction.

And the sound of eight people trying to get through a rather small door. And not all succeeding.

And the sound of a running beast the size of a kangaroo but greenish and with much bigger teeth trying to get in too –

'Hey!' said Rosetti, counting heads in the half-dark. 'Are we all here? Onyx!'

'Here.'

'Owen.'

'Here.'

'Miss Davies.'

'Here.'

'Mr Sartorius.'

'Here.'

'Trym.'

'Yea verily.'

'Otto.'

'Here.'

'Taxman Cosm.'

'Grrr.'

'Rraah.'

'Who's growling?' Pause, for counting heads. 'There are nine. One extra. Ooer. It's the kangaroo thing.'

'Help!' cried Otto.

'Aiee!' cried Cosm. The door burst open. The Headmaster-Designate and his Deputy rushed back into the Cretaceous. The kangaroo thing rushed after them, gnashing its awful teeth. 'Shut the door and lock it,' said Miss Davies. The light from outside was the colour of fire and blood. 'Three minutes to starfall.'

'Eek.' Everyone crowded on to the chair. Miss Davies picked up the dove prodder and prodded.

No flap, no squawk, no nests in the mind. Miss Davies pulled out the basket and checked.

'Whoops,' she said. 'Still asleep. Do something, Trym!'

'Mmyes!' said Trym, once again sucking air through his teeth in the manner of an Expert. 'They must awake naturally, or they will be too tired to travel. And we perish wyth alle lyfe on Erthe!'

'Do relax and talk properly,' said Miss Davies. 'We've got three minutes.'

'Two and a half,' said Owen.

'Thank you, Owen,' said Miss Davies, giving him her beautiful smile. '*Anything* can happen in two and a half minutes!'

10

A few minutes under 65 million years later, Founder's Day had dawned grey and rainy. Flags whipped from the summit of the Tower of Flight. The chamber pot placed by the Climbing Club on the topmost pinnacle had been removed. Strings of bunting criss-crossed the Quad. Pupils in their best clothes milled around, waiting for their parents, or the judges who had condemned them to the Skool, or officers from the various elite military squads that found Abbot Dagger's a great place to pick up tough recruits. The drawbridge was lowered, and on every hill in the Badlands armed guards had been posted.

At nine o'clock, a brilliant light winked from the heliograph station on the Edge.

'Ah,' said the Headmaster, reaching for his hairbrush and sweeping his hair up into something that looked like a white wave breaking. 'Here come the parents and so on. Nine more eggs and a glass of champagne for me nerves, and a good time to be had by all. Though I do wish,' he said, a cloud passing over his noble features, 'that they would hurry up with the Greyte Cup!'

In Mato's lair, Nurse Drax was keeping very still in case any part of her slipped. Her make-up was perfect. Her hair was lacquered into the texture of whipped granite, and her white cap of office was attached with hand-burnished brass pins. Her apron crackled with starch, and her brogues were polished so brightly that they reflected (had she but known it) her grubby pink wool knickers. 'Mmwah,' she said, blowing herself a sticky red kiss in the mirror. 'Mato, you are the very picture of beauty. By this day fortnight, you will be Madame Cosm!' She frowned. 'But where *is* everybody?'

The great clock in the Tower of Flight stood at ten to ten as the Headmaster swept down the steps at the east end of the Hall of Session. The Skool was milling around the floor, a mass of upturned faces shining with soap and expectation.

'Hail!' cried the Head.

'Hail, Head!' cried the Skool.

The Head's gaze swept the assembled staff. 'There do not seem to be enough masters.'

'All present except Dr Cosm and Otto –'

The Head broke into a genuine smile of delight –

'– and Davies and Sartorius.'

The Head's huge eyebrows drew together. 'Dear me,' he boomed. 'Ah, well. We will proceed without them. No doubt they will be back, ah, *in time*, haha.'

'Er,' said a Security Master. 'You are looking well nice, Headmaster. But –'

'Silence!' cried the Head. 'Now –'

'The robes, great, fabulous,' said the Security Master. 'But the pyjamas?'

The Head looked down. A striped knee heavily stained with cocoa looked back. By a perfectly ordinary oversight he had forgotten to put on his clothes. He had things on his mind. Such as why the Skolars had not shown up with the Cup. And how he was going to delay events to give them the best possible chance of doing it. Like a vast, silent engine, the great brain worked it all out, and came up with a solution. Delay. Delay was the only hope. 'Ah,' he said. 'I think we must have a revised timetable. Take this down, SM, and nail it to the Hall Door.'

The Head spoke. The Security Master wrote. Five minutes later the Skool crowded excitedly round the door.

10.00 Arrival and Reception of Governors and Visitors

10.30 Marching and Flag Display on Parade Ground

11.15 Massed choirs sing Skool Song
11.30 Speeches, Reports from Departments in Hall
   of Session
12.30 Fetching of Greyte Cup. Awarding of Cups
   in Hall of Session
13.00 Lunch
14.00 Exhibitions
18.00 Sunset
(signed)
S. Temple, Headmaster

'What about those doves?' said Onyx, fretting.

The noise outside was huge and horrible. Animals were roaring, trees were falling, rocks were rolling and lumps of the atmosphere were catching fire with a sound like extra large blowtorches.

'Still having their nap,' said Miss Davies, hiding a yawn with her beautiful fingers. 'Still, let us prepare ourselves for Time Travel. Eh, Trym?'

'We're all going to die,' whimpered that twisty servitor. 'Talk to your father, for pity's sake.'

Miss Davies closed her eyes. Then she opened them and shook her head. 'Not at home,' she said. 'I know! We'll sing the Skool Song.'

'Will that help?' said Trym.

'It will keep our spirits up,' said Miss Davies. 'Now. A-three, *four*!'

The brave voices of the pupils rose thin but tuneful in the roar of the collapsing planet. It seemed that something or someone was banging on the dovecote roof.

Probably Cosm, thought Rosetti. Or maybe Otto.

'Sing on!' cried Miss Davies. 'Sing on!'

Trapped in the Cretaceous, thirty seconds from Meteor Impact, the Polymathic Skolars of Abbot Dagger's Academy sang on.

The Skool clock struck ten. The Governors' steam bus rumbled over the drawbridge.

The gates swung open. The Skool was revealed, drawn up in ranks in the yard.

'Ugh,' said Commissioner Manacle.

'And here comes the Head,' said the Colonel. 'Strange trousers.'

'Ordinary trousers,' said Lady Squee. 'Back to front.'

'Genius,' said Inkon Stimp, R.A. 'Absent-minded, of course.'

'I'd rather he was just absent,' said the Colonel.

'Ha ha,' said the Commissioner.

'Ha ha,' said Lady Squee.

'Ha ha,' said Barry Duggan, scanning the crowd. 'Where's my boys?'

The steam bus stopped. A green light came on over the door.

'Ready?' said the Colonel. 'Out we go. But

where,' he said, in a low, puzzled bark, 'is Dr Cosm?'

Doctor Cosm was pretty close in space, but 65 million years away in Time, sitting on the roof of a tumbledown dovecote besieged by meat-eating dinosaurs in a burning cycad grove surrounded by erupting volcanoes into which a very large meteor was about to smash at fifty times the speed of sound.

'Ooer,' said Otto, as yellow teeth clashed by Cosm's foot.

'Throw a tile at it!' shrieked Cosm. '*At* it! Left a bit! Right a bit!'

'I'm doing my best,' said Otto sulkily, rubbing his throwing arm. '*You* throw something.'

'Me? Throw? I'm Headmaster Designate and soon to be Master of the Universe!'

'You look like lunch to that thing,' said Otto gloomily.

'Shut *up*!'

Lady Squee looked at the watch on her big hairy wrist. 'We are running late, I see.'

'Thirty-three minutes,' said Professor Tube, sniffing.

'Time is a fantasy,' said the Head in Ancient Egyptian.

'I beg your pardon?' said Tube. The Head

translated. 'This is not the view of Dr Cosm,' said Tube, sniffing wetly. 'Doctor Cosm is *punctual*.'

'Not today,' said the Head, with a hearty laugh.

Out in the Quad, the Skool waved flags, spelling out messages of greeting. HELLO GOVNERS, said the flags. WELKUM.

'Oh dear,' said the Head in English. 'Actually this flag stuff is under the direct supervision of Dr Cosm.'

'Woss the problem?' said Barry Duggan.

The sounds outside the dovecote were very loud indeed now. Also, it was getting hotter.

But this was not what was worrying Onyx.

'We're going to be so *late*!' she said. 'What will happen to the *Skool*?'

'And the Universe,' said Owen.

'Don't worry,' said Miss Davies, almost convincingly.

'That dove blinked!' cried Owen.

'I can sort of feel it coming back,' said Rosetti. 'It's got some way to go, though.'

'Which is more than you can say for that meteor,' said Owen. 'What did you say, Trym?'

'Just blubbering,' said Trym.

'Quite understandable,' said Rosetti, over the roar of cycads catching fire.

*

The Skool Song was sung:

'WE HAVE NOT BEEN VERY GOOD,' sang the
   Skool.
'WE HAVE NOT DONE RIGHT.
WE HAVE BEEN MISUNDERSTOOD
AND SET OUR SCHOOLS ALIGHT.
BUT OUR HEARTS ARE VERY HIGH,
PROUD AND CLEAN ARE WE.
O YES WE ARE HAPPY NOW
AT OUR AKADEMEE.
DAGGA DAGGA DAGGA DAGGA
SKOOL-A-SKOOL-A-SKOOL-A-SKOOL!'

'Goodness,' said Lady Squee, sticking her thick
fingers in her hairy ears.

'Barbaric,' said the Professor.

'Hmmph,' said the Colonel. 'What's next?'

'Speeches. You're first, Colonel.'

'Of course,' said the Colonel, looking pleased.
He groped in his pocket and pulled out a thick
wad of notes.

'Followed,' said the Head, 'by Awarding of Cups.
Then Lunch.'

'Ah!' said Lady Squee, Commissioner Manacle
and Barry Duggan.

'But do not hurry with your speech, Colonel,' said
the Head, looking furtively at his watch. 'Ononono
no. Tell us about the Soldier's Life. In detail.'

'Terribly boring,' said the Colonel, modestly but falsely.

'I know,' said the Head, who was feeling the suspense. He strode to the edge of the dais. 'RIGHT?' he bellowed.

'RIGHT!' bellowed the Skool.

'OK, Colonel, you're on,' said the Head, stepping back with the air of one introducing a doomed gladiator to the Roman Arena.

'Girls and boys, staff, parents and fellow Governors,' said the Colonel, pasting a smile to his face. 'Have you ever considered what Education really *is*?'

The staff, pupils, parents and Governors reached for packets of sweets, chewing gum and comics. They had not considered. They did not actually care.

It was going to be a long, long Founder's Day.

'One dove awake,' said Owen.

BOOM, went something outside, either a dinosaur leaping or a tree falling, nobody was going to check which. Thin screams from the roof.

'Another one's woken up!' said Onyx. 'And another! Oo!'

'Help,' said a voice on the roof.

'Who's that?' said Owen.

'Doctor Cosm,' said a thin, humble voice. 'And Otto.'

'Be quiet. We're trying to think.'

'Yes, Owen,' said Dr Cosm. 'Sorry you were troubled, Owen. Do you think you could possibly let us in, Owen?'

'No,' said Owen.

Roar, said the world outside. Howl, crunch.

'Bit of a personality change there,' said Rosetti. 'Now. You were saying?'

'We've got to go back almost all the way to Home Time and put the Cup back in the Sealed Room five minutes before it's time to collect it.'

'If enough doves wake up.'

'The first one's gone back to sleep.'

'Oh.'

'But look at those two!'

'They blinked! So did that one! We're off!'

'Ninthly,' the Colonel was saying, 'we must consider what to do with Johnny Foreigner. Johnny Foreigner is not like us . . .'

'He is foreign,' said a voice in the crowd.

'. . . he is foreign,' said the Colonel, who had not heard.

If anyone had been listening, they would no doubt have been rather shocked. Luckily, hardly anyone was. Cookery II had smuggled in a haunch of venison, which they were roasting over a bright fire of coals. Carpentry IX were putting the finishing touches to a ladder/bridge combination that they intended to use in a bold escape attempt should the speech go on till midnight. The Footerers had recovered their energy after the Old Boy's Bloodbath, and were getting restless.

'Tenthly,' said the Colonel –

'Gosh this is boring,' said the Head, unfortunately in English.

'Ffft,' said the Colonel, a pale steam of fury jetting from his ears.

''S'all right,' said Lady Squee, waking from a peaceful slumber with a creak of stressed tweed. 'He'll be gorn soon. And we'll have Dr Cosm instead. Barry's brought the contracts for sacking the silly old Head and signing up Cosm.'

'Too right,' said Barry Duggan.

'Dr *Cosm*!' cried Miss Davies merrily. 'What has *happened* to you?'

'Dunno,' said Dr Cosm in a strange, thin voice.

The dovecote was once again in its untidy corner of the Academy farmyard. The doves were sitting on the roof cooing. The children were breathing in the normal air and feeling delighted that they were not being extinguished by meteors, sacrificed in caves, drowned by floodwaters, looted by Vandals, burned in cathedrals, chopped up by French soldiers or having to smell the house of Abbot Dagger.

'Right. Rosetti, here's the Cup. Remember the opening instructions for the Sealed Room? Off you go, full speed!' cried Miss Davies. 'Onyx, spread the news! Owen, help her!' She waved to her departing Skolars, and turned to tidy up the dovecote.

'What about us?' said the oddly thin voice of Dr Cosm.

'What indeed?' said Miss Davies.

'I mean look at him,' said Dr Cosm, pointing at Otto.

'And look at *him*,' said Otto, pointing at Dr Cosm.

'Hmm,' said Miss Davies. As the two men stood in front of the dovecote door, she could see the keyhole through their bodies. 'You are a bit . . . well, see-through. I think part of you might have rubbed off on Time. In fact, you are timeworn.'

'I insist that you do something,' said Cosm.

'We could build you in to a house and use you as a window,' said Miss Davies.

'Or feed you lettuce seeds and use you as a mobile greenhouse,' said Wrekin Sartorius.

'*Brilliant!*' said Miss Davies.

Cosm cracked. 'Pity me!' he cried.

'Pleease,' said Otto.

'Ah!' said Miss Davies. 'The magic word!'

Wrekin Sartorius stepped back, frowning. 'I'll paint them,' he said.

'Wha?'

'They're see-through but solid,' said Wrekin. 'They just need filling in a bit.'

'You're brilliant,' said Miss Davies, looking at him with worshipping golden eyes.

'No, you are,' said Wrekin, looking back at her with adoring brown ones.

'No, you.'

'No, you.'

'If you have *quite* finished?' said Cosm.

Wrekin whipped out a portable paintbox and went to work on Cosm's flabby, half-visible features.

'One thing,' said Miss Davies.

'Hm?' said Dr Cosm.

'If anyone ever says you're no oil painting, they'll be right. But then again, they'll be wrong.'

'Boys and girls!' cried the Head. 'Put out your cooking fires, stop that brawling and enough of these speeches!' He turned a little pale. The hour had come: he could put it off no longer. He gazed out at the crowd, steeling himself for the worst. Then something caught his eye at the back. Something was bouncing. Onyx, with both her thumbs firmly up!

'Wahey!' cried the Head in Zulu, and did a handspring.

'Wha?' said the Colonel, scowling.

'Something marvellous has happened!' cried the Head. He smoothed his gown. 'It is time for the

Awarding of Cups. Ho for the Sealed Room,' he said, and set off. So rapid was his progress and so unmistakable his errand that the whole Skool followed him with a roar, the Skolars in the lead, until they stood in front of the monk's head.

'I make the Movements!' cried the Head. 'Look away.'

Everyone looked away. Though of course the Skolars knew perfectly well that he was taking the dagger from the monk's teeth, sticking it up the monk's right nostril, giving it a half turn, waiting for the mouth to fall open, grasping the tongue and pulling it sharply to the right, revealing –

'Atch*oo*!' cried Barry Duggan.

For the door had swung open, and from the chamber there had billowed an immense volume of choking dust.

'Wait!' cried the Head.

The Skool waited, not breathing, partly because of the suspense but mainly because of the dust.

Which settled.

And there in its case stood the Greyte Cup.

'I have great pleasure in awarding the Greyte Cup for Achievement!' cried the Head, back in the Hall of Session. 'The winners are . . . The Polymathic Skolars!'

'S'pose,' said the Governors.

'Eh, Dr Cosm?'

'Yes, of course, certainly,' said Dr Cosm meekly. He had a feeling that the white paint was peeling off his forehead, and he was terrified that someone would see what he was thinking.

'Er, Miss Davies?'

'Jolly good show,' said Miss Davies. Wrekin Sartorius nodded sulkily. He had just asked her to marry him, and she had refused.

'Hooray!' roared the Skool.

'Hooray!' piped Slee and Damage Duggan. Trym had rescued them from Time, but they had strange memories of being eaten by a *Tyrannosaurus maximperator*, and for some reason they were no good at Footer any more, and wanted to change their names to Tree and River and concentrate on quiet thoughts.

'So the hard part of Founder's Day is over!' cried the Head. 'Now is the time for sports, feasting and fireworks! And forward we go into the future, where anything may happen and certainly will! The first thing being my New Contract. Barry Duggan, pass it over!'

Barry Duggan passed it over. The Head signed with a flourish. 'I now declare a Whole Holiday!' he cried.

'HOORAAAH!' roared the pupils and teachers of Abbot Dagger's Academy for the Errant Children of the Absent.

*

Later, the Skolars sat in their Study, watching the firelight glow in the warm metal of the mystic Cup.

'Well,' said Miss Davies, 'we made it, and very proud of you I am too.'

'Miss Davies,' said Rosetti, 'we shall always be at your disposal to help save the Skool.'

'Or the Head's job.'

'Or the Universe,' said Owen.

'Oh, obviously,' said Miss Davies. 'But I don't think we'll do Time Travel again.'

'Ooooh,' groaned the Skolars. 'Why not?'

'Because this Cup is a force for Good. I think it chose the moments when it wanted to be found and hidden, so its absence was cancelled out by fires and wars and meteors, and it did not matter that sometimes it was present in two places at once. Feast your eyes on it while you can.'

The Skolars gazed deeply into its pure golden glow. And as they watched it faded, and was gone.

'Wha,' said Owen, his eyes crossing.

'It will have thought it best to return to the Sealed Room,' said Miss Davies. 'To await next Founder's Day, and perhaps someone else who wishes to take over the Skool and the Universe, whom it will defeat by sheer goodness. Now, then. We have done Time Travel. Anyone interested in Outer Space?'

Three hands shot up.

'Excellent,' said Miss Davies. 'Let us now turn our minds on how to get there.'

Puffin by Post

Abbot Dagger's Academy and the Quest for the Holy Grail

If you have enjoyed this book and want to read more,
then check out these other great Puffin titles.
You can order any of the following books direct with Puffin by Post:

Little Darlings • Sam Llewellyn • 9780141316918	£4.99
'Every now and then, a children's book comes along that is completely different. *Little Darlings* is one of these' – *Sunday Times*	

Bad Bad Darlings • Sam Llewellyn • 9780141317014	£4.99
'Fast-paced . . . hilarious. You'll love it' – *Mizz*	

Desperado Darlings • Sam Llewellyn • 9780141319810	£4.99
'Fabulously kooky' – *Sunday Times*	

The Return of Death Eric • Sam Llewellyn • 9780141318530	£5.99
The Sound of Music meets the School of Rock . . .	

The Haunting of Death Eric • Sam Llewellyn • 9780141319841	£5.99
He's back, and this time he's haunted . . .	

Just contact:

Puffin Books, C/o Bookpost, PO Box 29,
Douglas, Isle of Man, IM99 1BQ
Credit cards accepted. For further details:
Telephone: 01624 677237
Fax: 01624 670923

You can email your orders to: bookshop@enterprise.net
Or order online at: www.bookpost.co.uk

Free delivery in the UK.
Overseas customers must add £2 per book.

Prices and availability are subject to change.

Visit puffin.co.uk to find out about the latest titles, read extracts and
exclusive author interviews, and enter exciting competitions.
You can also browse thousands of Puffin books online.